# Five Nights at Freddy's

## FAZBEAR FRIGHTS #1
### INTO THE PIT

# Five Nights at Freddy's
## FAZBEAR FRIGHTS #1
### INTO THE PIT

SCOTT CAWTHON
ELLEY COOPER

Scholastic Inc.

If you purchased this book without a cover, you should be aware that this book is stolen property. It was reported as "unsold and destroyed" to the publisher, and neither the author nor the publisher has received any payment for this "stripped book."

Copyright © 2020 by Scott Cawthon. All rights reserved.

Photo of TV static: © Klikk/Dreamstime

Photos © Shutterstock: 82 and throughout (Winai Tepsuttinun), 89 and throughout (TheHighestQualityImages), 110, 146 (ZoranOrcik), 159, 180 (xpixel).

All rights reserved. Published by Scholastic Inc., *Publishers since 1920*. SCHOLASTIC and associated logos are trademarks and/or registered trademarks of Scholastic Inc.

The publisher does not have any control over and does not assume any responsibility for author or third-party websites or their content.

No part of this publication may be reproduced, stored in a retrieval system, or transmitted in any form or by any means, electronic, mechanical, photocopying, recording, or otherwise, without written permission of the publisher. For information regarding permission, write to Scholastic Inc., Attention: Permissions Department, 557 Broadway, New York, NY 10012.

This book is a work of fiction. Names, characters, places, and incidents are either the product of the author's imagination or are used fictitiously, and any resemblance to actual persons, living or dead, business establishments, events, or locales is entirely coincidental.

Library of Congress Cataloging-in-Publication Data available
ISBN 978-1-338-57601-6

10 9 8 7        22 23 24

Printed in the U.S.A.

First printing 2020 • Book design by Betsy Peterschmidt

# TABLE OF CONTENTS

```
Into the Pit . . . . . 1
To Be Beautiful . . . 68
Count the Ways . . . 138
```

# Five Nights at Freddy's

## FAZBEAR FRIGHTS #1
### INTO THE PIT

# INTO THE PIT

**T**he dead possum's still there." Oswald was looking out the passenger window at the gray, furry corpse on the side of the road. Somehow it looked even deader than it had yesterday. Last night's rain hadn't helped.

"Nothing looks deader than a dead possum," Oswald's dad said.

"Except this town," Oswald mumbled, looking at the boarded-up storefronts and the display windows, which were displaying nothing but dust.

"What's that?" Dad said. He was already wearing the stupid red vest they put him in when he worked the deli counter at the Snack Space. Oswald wished he'd wait to put it on until after he dropped him at school.

"This town," Oswald said, louder this time. "This town looks deader than a dead possum."

His dad laughed. "Well, I don't guess I can argue with that."

Three years ago, when Oswald was seven, there had actually been stuff to do here—a movie theater, a game and card store, and an ice-cream shop with amazing waffle cones. But then the mill had closed. The mill had basically been the reason the town existed. Oswald's dad had lost his job, and so had hundreds of other kids' moms and dads. Lots of families had moved away, including Oswald's best friend, Ben, and his family.

Oswald's family had stayed because his mom's job at the hospital was steady and they didn't want to move far away from Grandma. So Dad ended up with a part-time job at the Snack Space, which paid five dollars an hour less than he'd made at the mill, and Oswald watched the town die.

One business after another shut down, like the organs in a dying body, because nobody had the money for movies or games or amazing waffle cones anymore.

"Are you excited it's the last day of school?" Dad asked. It was one of those questions adults always asked, like "How was your day?" and "Did you brush your teeth?"

Oswald shrugged. "I guess. But there's nothing to do with Ben gone. School's boring, but home's boring, too."

"When I was ten, I wasn't home in the summer until I got called in for supper," Dad said. "I rode my bike and played baseball and got into all kinds of trouble."

"Are you saying I should get in trouble?" Oswald said.

"No, I'm saying you should have *fun*." Dad pulled into the drop-off line in front of Westbrook Elementary.

*Have fun.* He made it sound so easy.

Oswald walked through the school's double doors and ran smack into Dylan Cooper, the last person he wanted to see. Oswald was apparently the first person Dylan wanted to see, though, because his mouth spread in a wide grin. Dylan was the tallest kid in fifth grade and clearly enjoyed looming over his victims.

"Well, if it isn't Oswald the Ocelot!" he said, his grin spreading impossibly wider.

"That one never gets old, does it?" Oswald walked past Dylan and was relieved when his tormentor chose not to follow him.

When Oswald and his fifth-grade classmates were preschoolers, there was a cartoon on one of the little-kid channels about a big pink ocelot named Oswald. As a result, Dylan and his friends had started calling him "Oswald the Ocelot" on the first day of kindergarten and had never stopped. Dylan was the kind of kid who'd pick on anything that made you different. If it hadn't been Oswald's name, it would have been his freckles or his cowlick.

The name-calling had gotten much worse this year in U.S. history when they'd learned that the man who shot John F. Kennedy was named Lee Harvey Oswald. Oswald would rather be an ocelot than an assassin.

Since it was the last day of school, there was no attempt at doing any kind of real work. Mrs. Meecham had announced the day before that students were allowed to bring their electronics as long as they took responsibility for anything getting lost or broken. This announcement meant that no effort would be made toward any educational activities of any kind.

Oswald didn't have any modern electronics. True, there was one laptop at home, but the whole family shared it and he wasn't allowed to bring it to school. He had a phone, but it was the saddest, most out-of-date model imaginable, and he didn't want to take it out of his pocket because he knew any kid who saw it would make fun of how pathetic it was. So while other kids played games on their tablets or handheld consoles, Oswald sat.

After just sitting became intolerable, he took out a notebook and pencil and started to draw. He wasn't the best artist in the world, but he could draw well enough that his images were identifiable, and there was a certain cartoony quality about his drawings that he liked. The best thing about drawing, though, was that he could get lost in it. It was like he fell into the paper and became part of the scene he was creating. It was a welcome escape.

He didn't know why, but lately he had been drawing mechanical animals—bears, bunnies, and birds. He imagined them being human-size and moving with the jerkiness of robots in an old science-fiction movie. They were furry on the outside, but the fur covered a hard metal skeleton filled with gears and circuits. Sometimes he drew the animals' exposed metal skeletons or sketched them with the fur peeled back to show some of the mechanical workings underneath. It was a creepy effect, like seeing a person's skull peeking out from beneath the skin.

Oswald was so immersed in his drawing that he was startled when Mrs. Meecham turned off the lights to show a movie. Movies always seemed like a teacher's final act of desperation on the day before break—a way to keep the kids quiet and relatively still for an hour and a half before setting them loose for the summer. The movie Mrs. Meecham chose was, in Oswald's opinion, too babyish for a roomful of fifth graders. It was about a farm with talking animals, and he had watched it before, but he watched it again because, really, what else did he have to do?

At recess, kids stood around tossing a ball back and forth and talking about what they were going to do over the summer:

"I'm going to football camp."

"I'm going to basketball camp."

"I'm going to hang out at my neighborhood pool."

"I'm going to stay with my grandparents in Florida."

Oswald sat on a bench and listened. For him there would be no camps and no pool memberships and no trips because there was no money. And so he'd draw pictures, play his old video games that he'd already beaten a thousand times, and maybe go to the library.

If Ben were still here, it would be different. Even if they were just doing the same old stuff, they'd be doing it together. And Ben could always make Oswald laugh, riffing on video game characters or doing a perfect impersonation of one of their teachers. He and Ben had fun no matter what they did. But now a summer without Ben yawned before him, wide and empty.

Most days Oswald's mom worked from 12 p.m. until 12 a.m., so his dad had to make dinner. Usually they got by on frozen meals like lasagna or chicken potpie, or on cold cuts and potato salad from the Snack Space deli that were still good enough to eat but not good enough to sell. When Dad did cook, it was usually things that just required boiling water.

While Dad got their dinner ready, Oswald's job was to feed Jinx, their very spoiled black cat. Oswald often thought that he used about the same amount of cooking skill in opening Jinx's can of stinky cat food as his dad used in his dinner preparations.

Tonight Oswald and Dad were sitting down to plates of blue-box mac and cheese and some canned corn his dad had zapped in the microwave. It was a very yellow meal.

"You know, I was thinking," Dad said, squirting ketchup onto his macaroni and cheese. (*Why did he do that?* Oswald wondered.) "I know you're old enough to stay home by yourself some, but I don't like the idea of you staying by yourself the whole day while your mom and I are at work. I was thinking you could ride into town with me in the mornings and I could drop you off at the library. You could read, surf the net—"

Oswald couldn't let this one slide. How out of date could his dad be? "Nobody says 'surf the net' anymore, Dad."

"They do now . . . because I just said it." Dad forked up some macaroni. "*Anyway*, I thought you could hang out in the library in the mornings. When you get hungry, you could head over to Jeff's Pizza for a slice and a soda, and I could pick you up there once my shift's over at three."

Oswald considered for a moment. Jeff's Pizza was kind of weird. It wasn't dirty exactly, but it was run down. The vinyl on the booth seats had been repaired with duct tape, and the plastic letters had fallen off the menu board above the counter so the listed toppings included *pepperon* and *am urger*. It was clear that Jeff's Pizza used to be something bigger and better than it now was. There were tons of unused floor space and lots of unused electrical outlets along the base of the walls. Also, on the far wall was a small stage, even though there were no performances there, not even so much as a karaoke night. It was a strange place—sad and not what it had once been, like the rest of the town.

That being said, the pizza was decent, and more important, it was the only pizza in town if you didn't count the kind from the frozen food department at the Snack Space. The few good restaurants in town, including Gino's Pizza and Marco's Pizza (which, unlike Jeff's, had real pizza maker names), had closed their doors not long after the mill had.

"So you'll give me the money for pizza?" Oswald asked. Since Dad's job loss, Oswald's allowance had dwindled to practically nothing.

Dad smiled—a kind of sad smile, it seemed to Oswald. "Son, we're bad off, but we're not so bad off I can't spot you three-fifty for a slice and a soda."

"Okay," Oswald said. It was hard to say no to a warm, gooey cheese slice.

Since it wasn't a school night and wouldn't be again for quite some time, Oswald stayed up after Dad went to bed and watched an old Japanese monster movie, with Jinx curled up purring on his lap. Oswald had seen a lot of B-grade Japanese horror films, but this one, *Zendrelix vs. Mechazendrelix,* was new to him. As always, Zendrelix just looked like a giant dragon thing, but Mechazendrelix reminded him of the mechanical animals he drew when he stripped them of their fur. He laughed at the movie's special effects—the train Zendrelix destroyed was clearly a toy—and at how the actors' lip movements didn't match the dubbed-in English. Somehow, though, he always found himself rooting for Zendrelix. Even though he was just a guy in a rubber suit, somehow he managed to have a lot of personality.

In bed, he tried to count his blessings. He didn't have Ben, but he had monster movies and the library and lunchtime pizza slices. It was better than nothing, but it still wasn't going to be enough to keep him going all summer. *Please,* he wished, his eyes closed tight. *Please let something interesting happen.*

Oswald woke to the smell of coffee and bacon. The coffee he could do without, but the bacon smelled amazing.

Breakfast meant time with his mom, often the only time he got with her until the weekend. After one necessary stop, he hurried down the hall to the kitchen.

"Well, look at that! My rising sixth grader has risen!" Mom was standing over the stove in her fuzzy pink bathrobe, her blonde hair pulled back in a ponytail, flipping—oh, yum, were those pancakes?

"Hi, Mom."

She opened her arms. "I demand a morning hug."

Oswald sighed like it annoyed him, but he went over and hugged her. It was funny. With Dad, he always said he was too old for hugs, but he never turned down his mom's open arms. Maybe it was because he didn't get to spend much time with her during the week, while he and Dad spent so much time together they sometimes got on each other's nerves.

He knew Mom missed him and felt bad for having to work such long hours. But he also knew that since Dad's job at the Snack Space was just part-time, Mom's long hours were most of the reason the bills were getting paid. Mom always said that adult life was a fight between time and money. The more money you earned to spend on bills and necessities, the less time you got to spend with your family. It was a difficult balance.

Oswald sat down at the kitchen table and thanked his mom when she poured his orange juice.

"First day of summer break, huh?" Mom went back to the stove to scoop up a pancake with her spatula.

"Uh-huh." He probably should have tried to sound more enthusiastic, but he couldn't muster the energy.

She slid the pancake onto his plate and then served him two strips of bacon. "Not the same without Ben, huh?"

He shook his head. He wasn't going to cry.

Mom ruffled his hair. "I know. It's a bummer. But, hey, maybe a new friend will move to town."

Oswald looked at her hopeful face. "Why would anybody move here?"

"Okay, I see your point," Mom said, piling on another pancake. "But you never know. Or maybe somebody cool already lives here. Somebody you don't even know yet."

"Maybe, but I doubt it," Oswald said. "These pancakes are great, though."

Mom smiled and ruffled his hair again. "Well, I've got that going for me anyway. Do you want more bacon? If you do, you'd better grab it before your dad gets in here and vacuums it all up."

"Sure." It was Oswald's personal policy never to refuse more bacon.

The library was actually kind of fun. He found the latest book in a science-fiction series he liked and a manga that looked interesting. As always, he had to wait forever to use the computers because they were all taken by people who looked like they had no place else to be, men with scraggly beards wearing layers of ratty clothing, too-thin women with sad eyes and bad teeth. He waited his turn politely, knowing that some of these people used the library for shelter during the day, then spent the night on the streets.

Jeff's Pizza was as weird as he remembered. The big empty space beyond the booths and tables was like a dance floor where nobody danced. The walls were painted a pale yellow, but they must have used cheap paint or only one coat, because shapes of whatever had been on the walls before were still visible. It had probably been some kind of mural with people or animals, but now it was just shadows behind a thin veil of yellow paint. Oswald sometimes tried to figure out what the shapes were, but they were too blobby to make out.

Then there was the stage that never got used, standing empty but seemingly waiting for something. Though a feature even weirder than the stage lay in the back right corner. It was a large rectangular pen surrounded by yellow netting, but it had been roped off with a sign that said DO NOT USE. The pen itself was filled with red, blue, and green plastic balls that had probably been brightly colored once but were now faded and fuzzy with dust.

Oswald knew that ball pits had been popular features in kiddie playlands but had largely disappeared because of concerns about hygiene—after all, who was going to disinfect all those balls? Oswald had no doubt that if ball pits had still been popular when he was little, his mom wouldn't have let him play in one. As a licensed practical nurse, she was always happy to point out places she found to be too germy to play in, and when Oswald would complain that she never let him have any fun, she'd say, "You know what's not fun? Pinkeye."

Except for the empty stage and the ball pit, the strangest feature in Jeff's Pizza was Jeff himself. He seemed to be the only person who worked there, so he both took orders at the counter and made the pizzas, but the place was never crowded enough that this was a problem. Today, like all other days, Jeff looked as if he hadn't slept in a week. His dark hair was sticking up in weird places, and he had alarming bags under his bloodshot eyes. His apron was stained with both recent and ancient tomato sauce. "What can I getcha?" he asked Oswald, sounding bored.

"A cheese slice and an orange soda, please," Oswald said.

Jeff stared off into the distance as though he had to think about whether the request was a reasonable one or not. Finally he said, "Okay. Three-fifty."

One thing you could say about Jeff's pizza slices: They

were huge. Jeff served them on flimsy white paper plates that were soon stained with grease, and the corners of the triangles always overlapped the plates' rims.

Oswald settled in to a booth with his slice and soda. The first bite—the tip of the triangle—was always the best. Somehow the proportions of all the flavors in that bite were perfect. He savored the warm, melty cheese, the tangy sauce, and the pleasantly greasy crust. As he ate, he looked around at the few other customers. A pair of mechanics from the oil change place had folded up their pepperoni slices and were eating them like sandwiches. A table full of office workers clumsily attacked their slices with plastic forks and knives, so they wouldn't drip sauce on their ties and blouses, Oswald guessed.

After Oswald finished his slice, he wished for one more but knew he didn't have the money for it, so he wiped off his greasy fingers and took out his library book. He sipped his soda and read, falling into a world where kids with secret powers went to a special school to learn how to fight evil.

"Kid." A man's voice startled Oswald out of the story. He looked up to see Jeff in his sauce-stained apron. Oswald figured he had outstayed his welcome. He had sat in a booth reading for two hours after having bought a meal that cost less than four bucks.

"Yes, sir?" Oswald said, because politeness never hurt.

"I got a couple more cheese slices that didn't sell at lunch. You want 'em?"

"Oh," Oswald said. "No thanks, I don't have any more money." He wished he did, though.

"On the house," Jeff said. "I'd just have to throw 'em out anyway."

"Oh, okay. Sure. Thanks."

Jeff picked up Oswald's empty cup. "I'll get you some more orange soda while I'm at it."

"Thanks." It was funny. Jeff's expression never changed. He looked tired and miserable even when he was being extra nice.

Jeff brought two slices stacked on a paper plate, and a fresh cup of orange soda. "Here you go, kid," he said, setting down the cup and the plate.

"Thank you." Oswald wondered for a minute if Jeff felt sorry for him, if Jeff might think he was terribly poor like the homeless people who hung out all day in the library, instead of just the regular, barely-making-ends-meet poor that he was.

But then Oswald figured if there was free pizza sitting in front of you, maybe it wasn't time to worry about the reasons for it. Maybe it was time to eat.

Oswald had no problem polishing off the two huge slices. For the past month, his appetite had been unstoppable.

When Mom cooked him piles of pancakes in the morning, she said he must be having a growth spurt, causing him to eat like he had a hollow leg.

His phone vibrated in his pocket the second he sucked down the last of his soda. He looked at his dad's text: **will be out front at jeffs in 2 min.**

Perfect timing. It had been a good day.

The days at the library and Jeff's Pizza started to add up. The first couple of weeks had been great, but now the library didn't have the next book in the series he was reading, and he had grown bored with his online fantasy game, which, while advertised as free, now wouldn't let him advance any further without paying money. He had gotten tired of not having anybody his age to hang out with. He hadn't gotten tired of pizza yet, but he was starting to imagine that he might in the future.

Tonight was Family Fun Night, a one-night-a-week event that varied depending on Mom's work schedule. Back when the mill was still open, Family Fun Night meant dinner in a restaurant—pizza or Chinese or Mexican. After their meal, they'd do some fun activity together. They'd go to the movies if something kid friendly was playing, but if not, they'd go to the bowling alley or to the roller rink where Mom and Dad used to go on dates when they were in high school. Mom and Dad were great skaters and

Oswald was terrible, but they'd skate on either side of him holding his hands and keeping him up. They'd usually top off their evening with a waffle cone at the ice-cream place downtown. Oswald and Mom would make fun of Dad because no matter what ice-cream flavors were available, he always got vanilla.

Since the mill closed down, though, Family Fun Night had turned into an at-home affair. Mom would make something for dinner that was easy but festive, like tacos from a mix or hot dogs. They'd eat and then play board games or watch a movie they'd rented from Red Box. It was still fun, of course, but sometimes Oswald wished aloud for the old days of seeing new movies at the theater and having waffle cones after, and Dad had to remind him that the Important Thing Was That They All Got to Spend Time Together.

Sometimes when the weather was nice, they'd have a Family Fun Night. They'd pack a picnic of cold cuts and salads courtesy of the Snack Space and head over to the state park. They'd eat their dinner at a wooden table and watch the squirrels and birds and raccoons. Afterward, they'd go for a walk on one of the hiking trails. These outings were always a nice change, but Oswald was also aware of why these were the only Family Fun Nights that ever got them out of the house: Picnics were free.

Tonight they were staying in. Mom had made spaghetti and garlic bread. They had played a game of Clue, which Mom won as she usually did, and now they were piled up on the couch together in their pajamas with a huge bowl of popcorn between them, watching a remake of an old science-fiction movie.

Once the movie was over, Dad said, "Well, that was pretty good, but not as good as the real version."

"What do you mean, the real version?" Oswald said. "That was a real version."

"Not really," Dad said. "I mean, it was set in the same universe as the real version, but it was kind of a cheap knockoff of the one that came out when I was a kid."

Dad always had to be so opinionated. He could never just watch something and enjoy it. "So the best movies are always the ones that you watched when you were a kid?" Oswald said.

"Not always, but in this case, yes." Dad was settling in, Oswald could tell, for one of his favorite things: a good argument.

"But the special effects in the original version stink," Oswald said. "All those puppets and rubber masks."

"I'll take a puppet or model over CGI any day," Dad said, leaning back on the couch and propping his feet on the coffee table. "That stuff is so slick and fake. It's got no warmth, no texture. And besides, you like those old Zendrelix movies, and the special effects in those are terrible."

"Yeah, but I just watch those to make fun of them," Oswald said, even though he really did think Zendrelix was pretty cool.

Mom came in from the kitchen with bowls of ice cream. Not as good as the waffle cone place, but nothing to turn your nose up at, either. "Okay, if you guys don't cut out the nerd argument, I'm going to pick the next movie we watch. And it's going to be a *romantic comedy*."

Oswald and his dad shut up immediately.

"That's about what I thought," Mom said, passing around the bowls of ice cream.

As Oswald was lying in bed sketching his mechanical animals, his phone vibrated on his nightstand. There was only one person other than his parents who ever texted him.

**Hey,** Ben had typed on the screen.

**Heyback,** Oswald typed. **Hows your summer?**

**Awesome. At Myrtle Beach for vacation. Its so cool. Arcades and mini golf everywhere.**

**Jealous,** Oswald typed, and he meant it. A beach with arcades and mini golf really did sound awesome.

**Wish you were here,** Ben typed.

**Me too**

**Hows your summer**

**OK**, Oswald texted. He was briefly tempted to make his summer sound cooler than it was, but he could never lie to Ben. **Been going to the library a lot, lunch at Jeffs Pizza**

**Thats all?**

It did sound pathetic compared with a family trip to the beach. He texted, **Pretty much yeah**

**I'm sorry,** Ben texted, and then, **that pizza place is creepy**

They chatted a little while longer, and although Oswald was happy to hear from Ben, he was also sad that his friend was so far away and having such a good time without him.

Monday morning, and Oswald was in a bad mood. Even his mom's pancakes didn't help. In the car, Dad turned up the radio too loud. It was some stupid song about a tractor. Oswald reached for the knob and turned it down.

"Hey, dude, driver picks the music. You know that," Dad said. He turned the awful song back up even louder.

"It's bad music," Oswald said. "I'm trying to save you from yourself."

"Well, I don't like those video game songs you listen to," Dad said. "But I don't just barge into your room and turn them off."

"Yeah," Oswald said. "But I don't force you to listen to them, either."

Dad turned the radio down. "What's with the attitude, son? Whatever's bothering you, it's not just that I like country music."

Oswald didn't feel like talking, but clearly he was being forced to. And once he opened his mouth, he was surprised to feel complaints erupting from him like lava from a volcano. "I'm tired of every day being exactly the same. Ben texted me yesterday. He's at Myrtle Beach having an awesome time. He wanted to know what I was doing, and I told him I was going to the library and Jeff's Pizza every day, and you know what he texted back? 'I'm sorry' and 'That pizza place is creepy.'"

Dad sighed. "I'm sorry we can't go on vacation and have an awesome time, Oz. Things are hard right now where money's concerned. I'm sorry it affects you. You're a kid. You shouldn't have to worry about money. I'm hoping they'll move me to full time at the store in the fall. That'll help a lot, and if I get promoted to deli manager it'll be another dollar-fifty an hour."

Oswald knew he shouldn't say what he was about to say, but here he went anyway. "Ben's dad got a job that pays even better than his old job at the mill."

Dad tightened his grip on the steering wheel. "Yeah, well, and Ben's dad had to move five hundred miles away to get that job." His voice sounded tight, as tight as his grip on the wheel, and Oswald could tell his jaw was clenched. "Your mom and I talked a lot about it, but we decided not to move, especially with your grandma living here and needing help sometimes. This is our home, kiddo, and things aren't perfect, but we just have to make the best of them."

Oswald felt himself crossing the line from grumbling into grounding territory. But why did some people get the best of everything and others had to settle for free library visits and cheap pizza? "And so every day you toss me out on the street like garbage. If this is the best of things, I'd hate to see the worst!"

"Now, son, don't you think that's a little dramatic—"

Oswald didn't stick around to hear the rest of his dad's criticism. He got out of the car and slammed the door.

His dad sped away, probably glad to get rid of him.

Just as he predicted, the library still didn't have the book he wanted. He flipped through a few magazines—the kind with exotic jungle animals, which he usually liked, but they weren't doing much for him today. When his turn came for a computer, he put in his earbuds and watched some YouTube videos, but he wasn't in a good enough mood to laugh.

At lunchtime, he sat in Jeff's Pizza with his slice and soda. Every day, a cheese slice. If his dad wasn't so stingy, he'd give him another dollar so he could have pepperoni or sausage. But no, it had to be the cheapest pizza you could get. Sure, money was tight, but really, was another dollar a day going to break the bank?

Looking around the place, Oswald decided Ben was right. Jeff's Pizza was creepy. There were those shadowy painted-over figures on the walls, the dusty abandoned ball pit. And when he thought about it, Jeff was kind of creepy, too. He looked a hundred years old but was probably just thirty. With those heavy-lidded, bloodshot eyes, the stained apron, and the slow speech and movement, he was like a zombie pizza chef.

Oswald thought about his argument with Dad that morning. Soon Dad would be texting him, expecting him to come outside to the car. Well, today was going to be different. Today Dad would have to come and find him.

There was one perfect place to hide.

Oswald was going into the pit.

The pit was pretty gross, really. Obviously untouched for years, the plastic spheres were covered in a gray, fuzzy dust. But hiding there would be a great prank on his dad. His dad, who was always dropping him off and picking him up like somebody's dry cleaning, would actually have to get out of the car and make an effort for a change. Oswald wouldn't make it easy for him, either.

Oswald took off his shoes. Yes, the ball pit was disgusting, but at least getting into it would make today different from all the other days that had come before it.

He climbed into the pit and felt the balls parting to make room for his body. He moved his arms and legs. It was a little like swimming, if you could swim in dry plastic spheres. He found his footing at the bottom of the pit. Some of the balls were strangely sticky, but he tried not to think about why. If he was going to trick his dad, he was going to have to go all the way under.

He took a deep breath, as if he were about to jump into a swimming pool, and fell to his knees. That put him in up to his neck. Wiggling around so he was sitting on the pit's floor put his head under, too. The balls spread apart far enough that he could breathe, but it was dark and made him feel claustrophobic. The place stank of dust and mildew.

"Pinkeye," he could hear his mother's voice saying. "You're going to get pinkeye."

The smell really was getting to him. The dust tickled his nose. He felt a sneeze coming on, but he couldn't move his hand through the spheres fast enough to reach his nose and muffle it. He sneezed three times, each one louder than the one before.

Oswald didn't know if his dad was looking for him yet, but if he was, the sneezing ball pit had probably given away his location. Besides, it was too dark and too gross in there. He had to come up for air.

As he rose, his ears were assaulted by the sound of beeping electronics and yelling and laughing kids.

It took a few seconds for his eyes to adjust from the darkness of the pit to the brightness that now surrounded him, the flashing lights and vivid colors. He looked around and muttered, "Toto, I don't think we're in Kansas anymore."

The walls were lined with shiny arcade cabinets housing games he'd heard his dad talk about from his own childhood: *Ms. Pac-Man*, *Donkey Kong*, *Frogger*, *Q\*bert*, *Galaga*. A neon-lighted claw machine displayed plush blue elf-like creatures and orange cartoon cats. He looked down at the pit and realized he was surrounded by little kids wallowing in the strangely clean and now brightly colored plastic orbs. He stood over the preschoolers like a giant. He stepped out of the pit to find his shoes, but they were gone.

Standing on the colorful carpet in his sock feet, he looked around. There were lots of kids his age and younger, but there was something different about them. Everyone's hair was styled and fluffy, and the boys wore polo shirts in colors lots of guys wouldn't be caught dead in, like pink or aqua. The girls' hair was almost unbelievably big, with bangs that stood out from their foreheads like claws; they wore pastel-colored tops that matched their pastel-colored shoes. The colors, the lights, the sounds—it was sensory overload. And what was that music?

Oswald looked around to see where it was coming from. Across the room on a small stage, a trio of animatronic animals blinked their big blank eyes, opened and closed their mouths, and pivoted back and forth in sync with a jangly, annoying song. There was a brown bear, a blue rabbit with a red bow tie, and some kind of bird girl. They reminded Oswald of the mechanical animals he had caught himself drawing lately. The difference was that he could never decide if the animals in his drawings were cute or creepy.

These were creepy.

Strangely, though, the dozen or so little kids surrounding the stage didn't seem to think so. They were wearing birthday party hats with pictures of the characters on them, and dancing and laughing and having a great time.

When the smell of pizza hit Oswald's nose, he understood.

He was still in Jeff's Pizza, or more accurately, what Jeff's Pizza had been before Jeff took over. The ball pit was new and not roped off, all the outlets on the wall had arcade games plugged into them, and—he turned around to face the left wall. In the shapes of the shadows on the wall of Jeff's Pizza was a mural of the same characters "performing" on the stage: the brown bear, the blue rabbit, and the bird girl. Below their faces were the words FREDDY FAZBEAR'S PIZZA.

Oswald's insides turned to ice water. How had this happened? He knew where he was, but he didn't know *when* it was or how he got there.

Somebody bumped into him, and he jumped more than was normal. Since he felt the physical contact, this must not be a dream. He couldn't decide if this fact was good news or not.

"Sorry, dude," the kid said. He was about Oswald's age and he was wearing a light yellow polo with the collar turned up, tucked into what looked like a pair of dad jeans. The white tennis shoes he had on were huge, like clown shoes. He looked as if he had spent a long time fixing his hair. "Are you okay?"

"Yeah, sure," Oswald said. He wasn't sure he was okay actually, but he didn't know how to begin to explain his situation.

"I've not seen you here before," the kid said.

"Yeah," Oswald said, trying to figure out an explanation that wouldn't sound too weird. "I'm just visiting here . . . staying with my grandma for a few weeks. This place is great, though. All these old games—"

"*Old* games?" the kid said, raising an eyebrow. "You're joking, right? I don't know about where you're from, but

Freddy's has the newest games around here. That's why the lines to play them are so long."

"Oh yeah, I was just kidding," Oswald said, because he couldn't think of anything else to say. He had heard his dad talk about playing a lot of these games when *he* was a kid. Absurdly hard games, he said, on which he had wasted many hours and many quarters.

"I'm Chip," the kid said, running his fingers through his poofy hair. "Me and my buddy Mike"—he nodded at a tall black kid wearing huge eyeglasses and a shirt with wide red and blue stripes—"were about to play some Skee-Ball. Want to come with?"

"Sure," Oswald said. It was nice to hang out with some other kids, even if they seemed to be kids from another time. He didn't think this was a dream, but it sure was as weird as one.

"You got a name?" Mike said, looking at Oswald like he was some kind of strange specimen.

"Oh, sure. I'm Oswald." He had been too weirded out to remember to introduce himself.

Mike gave him a friendly slap on the back. "Well, I've gotta warn you, Oswald. I'm a beast at Skee-Ball. But I'll go easy on you since you're new here."

"Thanks for having mercy on me," Oswald said. He followed them to the Skee-Ball area. On the way they passed somebody in a rabbit suit that looked like a yellow version of the animatronic rabbit on the stage. Nobody else seemed to be paying attention to the rabbit guy, so Oswald didn't say anything. It was probably a Freddy Fazbear's employee dressed up to entertain the little kids at the birthday party.

Mike wasn't kidding about being a beast at Skee-Ball. He easily beat Chip and Oswald three times, but he was a good sport, and they spent the whole time joking around. It felt good being included.

But after another couple of games, Oswald started to worry. What time was it really? How long had his dad been looking for him? And how was he going to get back to his real life? Sure, he'd wanted to give Dad a little scare, but he didn't want to scare the old man so much he got the police involved.

"Hey, guys, I'd better run," Oswald said. "My grandma—" He almost said "just texted me" but realized Chip and Mike would have no idea what he was talking about. Whenever this was, there were no cell phones. "My grandma's supposed to pick me up in a few minutes."

"Okay, dude, maybe we'll catch you later," Chip said, and Mike gave a little nod and wave.

Oswald left his companions, stood in a corner in his sock feet, and wondered what to do. He was having some kind of magical experience, he was late getting back, and he was missing his shoes. He was like some kind of mixed-up guy Cinderella.

How to get back? He could walk out the front door of Freddy Fazbear's, but where would that take him? It might be the right place to find his dad's car waiting, but it wasn't the right time. Not the right decade, even.

Then it dawned on him. Maybe the way out was the same way he got in. At the ball pit, a mom was telling her two little kids it was time to leave. They tried to argue with her, but she turned on her Stern Mom Voice and threatened them with an early bedtime. Once they got out, he got in.

He sank beneath the surface before anybody could see that a kid over the height limit was in the ball pit. How long to stay under? Randomly, he decided to count to one hundred, then stand.

He rose to his feet and found himself standing in the dusty, roped-off ball pit at Jeff's Pizza. He climbed out and found his shoes right where he'd left them. His phone vibrated in his pocket. He took it out and read, **Will be there in 2 min.**

Had no time passed at all?

He headed out the door, and Jeff called, "See ya, kid" behind him.

"This looks great, Mom," Oswald said, spearing a sausage link with his fork.

"You're in a good mood today." Mom slid a waffle onto his plate. "Quite a contrast from yesterday when you were Mr. Grumpy Pants."

"Yeah," Oswald said, "they're supposed to get my book in the library today." This statement was true, but it wasn't the reason Oswald was in a good mood. Of course it wasn't like he could tell her the real reason. If he said, "I discovered a ball pit at Jeff's Pizza that lets me travel in time," Mom would be dropping the waffles and picking up the phone to call the nearest child psychologist.

Oswald picked up his book at the library but was too impatient to read it. He headed over to Jeff's Pizza as soon as it opened at eleven.

Jeff was in the kitchen when he got there, so he made a beeline for the pit.

He shucked off his shoes, stepped in, and sank into the depths. Since it had seemed to work before, he counted to one hundred before he stood.

The animatronic band was "playing" some weird jangly song that was partially drowned out by the beeping, blipping, and dinging of a variety of games. He wandered the floor and took in the video games, the Whac-A-Mole, the neon-lighted token suckers that let you win some tickets (but probably not) if you pushed the button at the right time. Older kids crowded around the video games. Preschoolers climbed on the crayon-colored play equipment. *Pinkeye,* Oswald thought, though he had no room to talk, the way he was diving into the ball pit these days.

Everything looked as it had before. He had even caught sight of a calendar hanging in an open office that helped him pinpoint the date: 1985.

"Hey, it's Oswald!" Chip was wearing a baby-blue polo with his dad jeans and giant sneakers this time. Not a hair on his head was out of place.

"Hey, Oz," Mike said. He was wearing a *Back to the Future* T-shirt. "Anybody ever call you that—like the Wizard of Oz?"

"They do now," Oz said, grinning. He had gone from having the loneliest summer ever to having two new friends—and a nickname. True, all of these seemed to be happening in the mid-1980s, but why get hung up on the details?

"Hey," Chip said, "we just ordered a pizza. You want to come have some? We ordered a large, so there's more than we can eat."

"Speak for yourself," Mike said, but he was grinning.

"Okay," Chip said, "how about I say it's more than we *should* eat? Wanna join us?"

Oswald was curious how Freddy Fazbear's pizza compared with Jeff's. "Sure. Thanks."

On the way to their table, they passed someone in

that same yellow rabbit suit who was standing in a corner, still as a statue. Chip and Mike either didn't see him or ignored him, so Oswald tried to ignore him as well. Why hide in the corner like that, though? If he worked for the restaurant, surely he wasn't supposed to act all creepy.

At the table, a young woman with big blonde hair and blue eye shadow served them a large pizza and a pitcher of soda. In the background, the animatronic band played on. The pizza was pepperoni and sausage with a crispy crust, a nice change from plain cheese slices.

"You know," Mike said between bites, "when I was little, I loved Freddy Fazbear's band. I even had a stuffed Freddy I used to sleep with. Now I look up at that stage and those things give me the creeps."

"It's weird, huh? How stuff you like as a little kid gets creepy when you're older?" Chip helped himself to another slice. "Like clowns."

"Yeah, or dolls," Mike said between bites. "Sometimes I look at my sister's dolls all lined up on the shelf in her room, and it's like they're staring at me."

*Or like that guy in the yellow rabbit costume,* Oswald thought, but he didn't say anything.

After they demolished the pizza, they played some Skee-Ball, Mike mopping the floor with them again but being really nice about it. Oswald didn't worry about time anymore, because apparently time here didn't pass the same way as in his own time zone. After Skee-Ball, they took turns playing air hockey in pairs. Oswald was surprisingly decent at it and even managed to beat Mike once.

When they started to run low on tokens, Oswald thanked them for sharing their wealth and said he hoped to see them again soon. After they said their good-byes, Oswald waited until no one was looking and disappeared into the pit.

Hanging out with Chip and Mike turned into a regular thing. Today they weren't even playing games. They were just sitting at a booth, drinking sodas and talking, trying to ignore the animatronic animals' annoying music as much as they could.

"You know what movie I liked?" Chip said. His polo shirt was peach-colored today. Oswald loved the guy, but really, didn't he own one shirt that wasn't the color of an Easter egg? "*The Eternal Song.*"

"Seriously?" Mike said, pushing his huge glasses up on his nose. "That movie was so boring! I was like, *The Eternal Song* is the perfect title for this movie because I don't think it's ever going to end!"

They all laughed, and then Chip said, "What did you think of it, Oz?"

"I haven't seen that one," Oswald said. He said that a lot when hanging out with Chip and Mike.

Oswald always listened to them talk about movies and shows they liked. When they mentioned one he didn't know, he'd look it up online when he got home. He made a list of '80s movies he wanted to watch and checked the TV listings on the DVR to see when any of them might be showing. Oswald participated in Chip and Mike's conversations as much as he could. It was kind of like being a foreign exchange student. He sometimes had to fake his way through by smiling and nodding and being generally agreeable.

"Man, you need to get out more," Mike said. "Maybe you can go to the movies with Chip and me sometime."

"That'd be cool," Oswald said, because what else could he say? *Actually, I'm from the distant future, and I don't think it's physically possible for me to see you anyplace but in Freddy Fazbear's in 1985.* They'd both think that was a joke on Mike because his favorite movie was *Back to the Future*.

"Name one movie you've seen that you really like," Chip said to Oswald. "I'm trying to figure out what your taste is."

Oswald's mind went blank. What was a movie from the '80s? "Uh . . . *E.T.*?"

"*E.T.*?" Mike slapped the table, laughing. "*E.T.* was, like, three years ago. You really do need to get out more! Do they not have movie theaters where you come from?"

*They do,* Oswald thought. *And they have Netflix and*

*PlayStation and YouTube and social media.* But he didn't say it.

Of course there was technology Chip and Mike talked about that he had only the vaguest knowledge of, like VCRs and boom boxes and cassette tapes. And he constantly had to remind himself not to talk about things like cell phones and tablets and the internet. He tried not to wear T-shirts with characters and references that might confuse them or the other customers at 1985 Freddy Fazbear's.

"Yeah, we definitely need to bring you up to date," Chip said.

*If you only knew,* Oswald thought.

"Hey, do you want to go play some games?" Mike said. "I feel the Skee-Ball calling me, but I promise I'll go easy on you guys."

Chip laughed. "No, you won't. You'll murder us."

"You guys go ahead," Oswald said. "I think I'll just stay at the table."

"What, and watch the show?" Mike said, nodding in the direction of the creepy characters on the stage. "Is something wrong? If you've suddenly decided you like Freddy Fazbear's music, we need to get you help fast."

"No, nothing's wrong," Oswald said, but really, something was. For his first few visits to 1985 Freddy Fazbear's, it hadn't even occurred to him that he was basically mooching off Chip and Mike's generosity because he never had any money of his own. And even if he wasn't broke in his own time zone, would the money he brought from the present day even work in 1985? It was kind of pitiful, being broke in two decades.

Finally he said, "I just feel like I'm always taking your money because I never have any."

"Hey, dude, it's cool," Chip said. "We hadn't even noticed."

"Yeah," Mike said, "we just figured your grandma never gave you any money. I know my grandma doesn't except when it's my birthday."

They were being really nice, but Oswald still felt embarrassed. If they had talked about his lack of money, that meant they had noticed it. "How about I just go hang out with you while you play?" Oswald said.

When he stood up, he felt a strange heaviness in his pockets. Something in them was so heavy he felt like his jeans might fall down. He reached in his pockets and pulled out double handfuls of 1985 Freddy Fazbear's game tokens. He produced handful after handful and dumped them on the table. "Or we could all play using these," he said. He had no idea how to explain the magic that had just occurred. "I guess I forgot I was wearing these pants . . . the ones that had all the tokens in them."

Chip and Mike looked a little confused, but then they grinned and started raking coins from the table into their empty soda cups.

Oswald did the same. He decided just to go with the weirdness. He didn't know how the tokens got there, but then again, he didn't really know how *he* got there, either.

In the morning, as Dad was driving him to the library, Oswald asked, "Dad, how old were you in 1985?"

"I was just a couple years older than you," Dad said. "And other than baseball, all I could think about was how many quarters I had to spend at the arcade. Why do you ask?"

"No reason in particular," Oswald said. "I've just been doing some research. Jeff's Pizza—back before it was Jeff's Pizza, it was some kind of arcade, wasn't it?"

"Yeah, it was." Dad's voice sounded strange, nervous maybe. He was quiet for a few seconds, then said, "But it closed."

"Like everything else in this town," Oswald said.

"Pretty much, yeah," Dad said, pulling up in front of the library.

Maybe it was Oswald's imagination, but it seemed like his dad was relieved to get to their destination so he wouldn't have to answer any more of his questions.

At eleven o'clock sharp, Oswald headed over to Jeff's Pizza, as had become his habit. With Jeff nowhere in sight, Oswald proceeded to the pit. After his count to one hundred, he stood. There were noises but not the usual ones of Freddy Fazbear's. Screams. Crying children. Yells for help. The fast footfalls of people running. Chaos.

Were Chip and Mike here? Were they okay? Was anybody here okay?

He was afraid. Part of him wanted to disappear back into the pit, but he was worried about his friends. Also, he was burning with curiosity about what was going on, even though he knew whatever it was, it was horrible.

He wasn't in danger, he told himself, because this was the past, a time way before he was born. His life couldn't be in danger in a time before he even existed, could it?

His stomach in knots, he moved through the crowd, past crying mothers running with their toddlers in their arms, past dads grasping children's hands and leading them swiftly toward the exit, their faces masks of shock.

"Chip? Mike?" he called, but his friends were nowhere to be seen. Maybe they hadn't come to Freddy Fazbear's today. Maybe they were safe.

Scared but feeling as if he had to know what was happening, Oswald walked in the opposite direction from everyone else with an escalating feeling of dread.

In front of him stood the man in the yellow bunny costume . . . if it was a man under there. The bunny opened a door that said PRIVATE and went inside.

Oswald followed.

The corridor was long and dark. The rabbit looked at him with blank eyes and an unchanging grin, then walked farther down the hall. Oswald wasn't chasing the rabbit. He was letting the rabbit lead him, as if he were in a terrifying version of *Alice in Wonderland*, going down the rabbit hole.

The rabbit stopped in front of a door with a sign reading PARTY ROOM and beckoned for Oswald to come inside. Oswald was shaking with terror, but he was too curious to refuse. *Besides,* he kept thinking, *you can't hurt me. I haven't even been born.*

Once inside the room, it took Oswald a few seconds to register what he was actually seeing and a few more seconds for his brain to process it.

They were lined up against the wall, which was painted with images of the place's mascots: the grinning bear, the blue bunny, and the bird girl. Half a dozen kids, none of them older than Oswald, their lifeless bodies propped into sitting positions, their legs stretched out in front of them. Some of them had their eyes closed as if asleep. Others' eyes were open, frozen in an empty, doll-like stare.

They were all wearing Freddy Fazbear birthday party hats.

Oswald couldn't tell how they had died, but he knew the rabbit was responsible for it, that the rabbit had wanted him to see his handiwork. Maybe the rabbit wanted

Oswald to be his next victim, to join the others lined up against the wall with their unseeing eyes.

Oswald screamed. The yellow rabbit lunged for him, and he ran out of the room and down the black corridor. Maybe the rabbit could hurt him; maybe he couldn't. Oswald didn't want to hang around long enough to find out.

He ran across the now-empty arcade toward the ball pit. Outside, the police sirens' screams matched Oswald's own. The rabbit ran after him, getting so close that a fuzzy paw brushed Oswald's back.

Oswald dove into the pit. He counted to one hundred as fast as he could.

When he stood, the first thing he heard was Jeff's voice. "There's the little stinker!"

Oswald turned to see his dad stomping toward him while Jeff looked on. Dad looked furious, and Jeff didn't look happy, either—not that he ever did.

Oswald stood frozen, too overwhelmed to move.

His dad grabbed his arm and pulled him out of the pit. "What were you thinking hiding in that nasty old thing?" Dad said. "Didn't you hear me calling you?"

After Oswald was out, his dad leaned over the pit. "Look at how dirty this is. Your mother—"

A pair of yellow arms reached out of the pit and pulled Dad under.

The struggle would have been cartoonish if it hadn't been so terrifying. Dad's feet in their brown work boots kicked up to the surface, only to disappear below, then a pair of big fuzzy yellow feet appeared, only to disappear, too. The balls in the pit roiled like a stormy sea, and then they were still. The yellow rabbit rose from the pit, adjusted his purple bow tie, brushed off his front, and turned toward Oswald, grinning.

Oswald backed away, but the rabbit was beside him, its arm firmly around Oswald's shoulders, guiding him toward the exit.

Oswald looked at Jeff, who stood behind the counter. Maybe Jeff would help him? But Jeff wore the same hang-dog expression he always wore and just said, "See you later, guys."

How could Jeff—how could anyone—act like this situation was normal?

Once the rabbit got him outside, it opened the passenger door of Dad's car and pushed Oswald in.

Oswald watched as the bunny buckled its seat belt and started the car. He tried to open the door, but the bunny had activated the power lock from the driver's side.

The bunny's mouth was frozen in a rictus grin. Its eyes stared blankly.

Oswald pushed the unlock button again even though he knew it wouldn't work. "Wait," Oswald said. "Can you do any of this? Can you even drive a car?"

The bunny said nothing but started the car and pulled it into the street. It stopped at a red light, so Oswald figured it must be able to see and must know the basic rules of driving.

"What did you do to my dad? Where are you taking me?" Oswald could hear the panic in his voice. He wanted to sound strong and brave, like he was standing up for himself, but instead he just sounded scared and confused. Which he was.

The bunny said nothing.

The car made a familiar right turn, then a familiar left into Oswald's neighborhood.

"How do you know where I live?" Oswald demanded.

Still silent, the bunny turned into the driveway in front of Oswald's ranch-style house.

*I'll run for it,* Oswald thought. *As soon as this thing unlocks the car door, I'll run to a neighbor's house and call the police once I'm safely inside.* The locks clicked, and Oswald jumped out of the car.

Somehow the bunny was standing right in front of him. It grabbed his arm. He tried to break free, but its grip was too strong.

The bunny dragged Oswald to the front door, then yanked off the chain around Oswald's neck that held his house key. The rabbit turned the key in the door and shoved Oswald inside. Then it stood in front of the door, blocking the exit.

Jinx the cat wandered into the living room, took one look at the rabbit, arched her back, puffed out her tail, and hissed like a cat on a Halloween decoration. Oswald had never seen her act scared or unfriendly before, and he watched as she turned tail and fled down the hall. If Jinx knew this situation was bad, it must be really bad.

"You can't do this," Oswald said to the rabbit, in tears. He didn't want to cry. He wanted to look strong, but he couldn't help it. "This—this is kidnapping or something! My mom will be home soon, and she'll call the police."

It was a total bluff, of course. Mom wouldn't be home until after midnight. Would he even be alive by the time Mom got home? Was his dad even alive now?

He knew the bunny would grab him if he tried to make a run for the back door. "I'm going to my room now, okay? I'm not trying to escape. I'm just going to my room." He backed away, and the bunny let him. As soon as he got inside his room, he slammed the door and locked it. He took deep breaths and tried to think. There was a window in his room, but it was high and too small to climb through. Under his bed, Jinx let out a low growl.

Oswald could hear the bunny outside his door. If he

made a phone call, it would hear him. But maybe he could send a text.

He took out his phone and with shaking hands texted: **Mom, emergency! Somethings wrong with dad. Come home now**

Oswald knew even as he texted that she wouldn't be coming home now. Because she was always dealing with medical emergencies at work, sometimes it took her a long time to check her phone. It was Dad who Oswald was supposed to contact in the event of an emergency. But obviously that wasn't going to work now.

A miserable hour passed until Oswald's phone vibrated. Afraid the rabbit might still be listening outside his locked door, he picked up without saying hello.

"Oswald, what's going on?" Mom sounded terrified. "Do I need to call nine one one?"

"I can't talk now," Oswald whispered.

"I'm on my way home, okay?" She hung up.

Fifteen minutes seemed to pass more slowly than Oswald thought was possible. Then there was a knock on Oswald's door.

Oswald jumped, his heart in his throat. "Who is it?"

"It's me," Mom said, sounding exasperated. "Open the door."

He opened the door just a crack to make sure it was

really her. Once he let her in, he closed and locked the door behind them.

"Oswald, you need to tell me what's going on." Mom's brow was furrowed with worry.

Where to start? How to explain without sounding crazy? "It's Dad. He's . . . he's not okay. I'm not even sure where he is—"

Mom put her hands on both his shoulders. "Oswald, I just saw your dad. He's lying on the bed in our bedroom watching TV. He made you a chicken potpie for dinner. It's sitting on the stove."

"What? I'm not hungry." He tried to wrap his mind around his mom's words. "You saw Dad?"

Mom nodded. She was looking at him like he was one of her patients instead of her kid, like she was trying to figure out what was wrong with him.

"And he's okay?"

She nodded again. "He's okay, but I'm worried about you." She put her hand on his forehead as if checking for a fever.

"I'm okay," Oswald said. "I mean, if Dad's okay, I'm okay. He just . . . didn't seem okay."

"Maybe it's good school's starting back. I think you're spending too much time by yourself."

What could he say? *Actually, I've been spending time with*

*my new friends in 1985*? "Maybe so. I probably should just go on to bed. I have to get an early start in the morning."

"I think that's a good idea," Mom said. She put her hands on his cheeks and looked him directly in the eyes. "And listen, if you're going to text me at work, make sure it's a real emergency. You scared me."

"I thought it was a real emergency. I'm sorry."

"It's all right, honey. Get some rest, okay?"

"Okay." After Mom left, Oswald looked under the bed. Jinx was still there, crouched in a ball like she was trying to make herself as small and invisible as possible, her eyes wide and looking terrified. "It's okay, Jinxie," Oswald said, reaching under the bed and wiggling his fingers at her. "Mom says it's safe. You can come out now."

The cat wouldn't budge.

Oswald lay awake in bed. If Mom said Dad was there and okay, then it must be true. Why would she lie?

But Oswald knew what he had seen.

He had seen the yellow thing, as he had started to think of it, drag his dad into the pit. He had seen the yellow thing climb out of the pit, had felt its grip on his arm, sat beside it in the car as it drove him home.

Or had he? If Mom said Dad was home and okay, he must be. Oswald trusted his mom. But if Dad was okay, it meant Oswald hadn't seen what he thought he saw. And that must mean that Oswald was losing his mind.

After only a few hours of fitful sleep, Oswald woke to the aroma of frying ham and baking biscuits. His stomach rumbled, reminding him he had missed dinner last night.

Everything felt normal. Maybe he should just treat yesterday like a bad dream and try to move forward. A new school year, a new beginning.

He stopped in the bathroom, then made his way to the kitchen.

"Feeling better?" Mom asked. There she was, her hair in a ponytail, wearing her pink fuzzy bathrobe, fixing breakfast just like always. Something about this fact made Oswald feel tremendously relieved.

"Yeah," he said. "I'm pretty hungry, actually."

"Now that's a problem I can fix," Mom said. She set down a plate with two ham biscuits on it and poured him a glass of orange juice.

Oswald ate the first ham biscuit in three big bites.

The yellow thing walked in and sat across from him at the breakfast table.

"Uh . . . Mom?" Oswald's heart beat like a jackhammer in his chest. The ham biscuit sat heavy in his churning stomach.

"What is it, hon?" Her back was turned as she fiddled with the coffeemaker.

"Where's Dad?"

She turned around, the coffeepot in her hand. "Oswald,

your dad is sitting right across from you! If this is some kind of elaborate prank, you can cut it out right now because it has officially stopped being funny." She poured a cup of coffee and set it down in front of the yellow thing, which stared straight ahead, its mouth set in an unchanging grin.

Oswald knew he wasn't getting anywhere. Either he was insane or his mom was. "Okay, I understand. I'll cut it out. I apologize. May I be excused so I can get ready for school?"

"Of course," Mom said, but she was looking at him kind of funny again.

Oswald stopped in the bathroom to brush his teeth and then went to his room to get his backpack. He peeked under his bed to find Jinx still hiding there. "Well, it's good to know there's somebody else in this family who has some sense," he said. When Oswald came back into the kitchen, the yellow thing was standing by the door, car keys in its paw.

"Is . . . uh . . . Dad taking me to school?" Oswald asked. He didn't know if he could bear sitting beside it in the car again, hoping it was watching the road as it stared through the windshield with its empty eyes.

"Doesn't he always?" Mom said. He could hear the worry in her voice. "Have a good day, okay?"

Seeing no choice, Oswald got in the car beside the yellow thing. Once again, it locked all the doors from the driver's side. It backed out of the driveway and passed a jogging neighbor, who waved at it just as if it were his dad.

"I don't understand," Oswald said, on the edge of tears. "Are you real? Is this real? Am I going crazy?"

The yellow thing said nothing, just stared at the road ahead.

When it pulled up in front of Westbrook Middle School, the crossing guard and the kids at the crosswalk didn't seem to notice that the car was being driven by a giant yellow rabbit.

"Hey," Oswald said before he got out of the car, "don't bother picking me up this afternoon. I'll just catch the bus."

The school bus was a big yellow thing he could handle.

Because it was some kind of cosmic law, the first person Oswald saw in the hall was Dylan, his tormentor. "Well, well, well, if it isn't Oswald the Oc—"

"Give it a rest, Dylan," Oswald said, pushing past him. "I've got way bigger problems than you today."

It was impossible to concentrate in class. Usually Oswald was a pretty decent student, but how could he focus with his life and possibly his sanity falling apart? Maybe he should talk to someone, the school counselor or the school police officer. But he knew anything that came out of his mouth would sound dangerously crazy. How could he convince a police officer that his dad was missing if everybody who looked at the yellow thing saw Oswald's dad?

There was no one to help him. Oswald was going to have to figure out how to solve this problem himself.

At recess he sat on a bench by the playground, grateful that he didn't have to pretend to listen to a teacher and could just think. He couldn't imagine how his life could get any weirder. The yellow thing seemed to think it was his father. This was weird enough, but why did everybody else think it was his father, too?

"Do you mind if I share your bench?" It was a girl Oswald had never seen before. She had curly black hair and big brown eyes and was holding a thick book.

"Sure, help yourself," Oswald said.

The girl sat on the opposite end of the bench and opened her book. Oswald went back to his confused, confusing thoughts.

"Have you gone to this school for a long time?" the girl asked him after a few minutes. She didn't look over at Oswald when she talked; she just kept staring at the pages of her book. Oswald wondered if this meant she was shy.

"Since kindergarten," Oswald said, and then, because he couldn't think of a single other thing to say about himself, he asked, "What are you reading?"

"Greek mythology," she said. "Tales of heroes. Have you read much mythology?"

"No, not really," he said, feeling stupid immediately after. He didn't want to give the impression that he was the kind of guy who never read books. In desperation, he added, "I love to read, though," and then he felt even stupider.

"Me too," she said. "I've probably read this book a dozen times. It's like a comfort book for me. I read it when I need to be brave."

The word *brave* struck a chord in Oswald. Brave was what he needed to be, too. "Why's that?"

"Well, the Greek heroes are super brave. They're always doing battle with some kind of big monster, like the minotaur or the hydra. It kind of puts things in perspective, you know? No matter how bad my problems are, at least I don't have to do battle with a monster."

"Yeah," Oswald said, even though he was trying to figure out how to do battle with a monster—a yellow, long-eared monster—in his own home. He couldn't tell this girl about the yellow thing, though. She would think he was crazy and would be leaving their shared bench in a hurry. "So you said you read that book when you need to be brave." He was surprised he was having this conversation given the way his mind was racing. For some reason, this girl was easy to talk to. "I mean, it may be none of my business, but I was wondering why you needed to . . . to be brave."

She gave a shy little smile. "First day at a new school, third day in a new town. I don't know anybody yet."

"Yes, you do," he said. He held out his hand. "I'm Oswald." He didn't know why he was offering his hand like he was some kind of businessman, but it felt like the right thing to do.

She took his hand and shook it surprisingly firmly. "I'm Gabrielle."

Somehow, this was the conversation Oswald had needed to have.

He took the bus home from school. When he came inside, the yellow thing was vacuuming the living room.

He didn't ask it any more questions. It wasn't as if it could give him any answers anyway, and besides, if he was going to make his plan work, he was going to have to act like everything was normal. And as anybody who had seen him in the fourth-grade class play knew, acting was not one of his talents.

Instead, he did what he was supposed to do when life was normal, when his real dad was vacuuming the living room. He got the feather duster out of the cleaning closet and dusted the coffee table, the end tables, and the lamps. He emptied the wastebasket and neatened the throw pillows on the couch. Then he went to the kitchen and took out the garbage and the recycling. Once he was outside, it was tempting to run, but he knew running was not the answer. If everybody saw the yellow thing as his dad, nobody would help him.

The yellow thing would always catch him.

He went back inside.

His chores done, he walked right past the yellow thing. "I'm gonna go chill out a while before dinner," he said, even though the possibility of relaxing in any way was unimaginable. He went to his room, but he didn't close the door. Instead, he took off his shoes, sprawled on the bed, and started drawing in his sketchbook. He didn't want to draw mechanical animals, but they seemed to be all he could draw. He shut his sketchbook and started reading a manga, or at least pretending to. Normal. The plan could only work if he acted like everything was normal.

When the rabbit appeared in his doorway, he managed not to gasp. It beckoned for him the same way it had when it led him into the murder room at Freddy Fazbear's, and he followed it into the kitchen. On the table was one of the grocery store pizzas his dad kept in the freezer, baked to a pleasing golden brown, and two glasses of the fruit punch Oswald liked. The pizza had already been sliced, which was a relief, because Oswald couldn't imagine what he would have done if he had seen the thing holding a knife. Run screaming out into the street, probably.

Oswald sat down at the table and helped himself to a

slice of the pizza. He didn't feel much like eating, but he knew he couldn't act like anything was wrong. He took a bite of pizza, a sip of punch. "Aren't you going to eat anything . . . Dad?" he asked. It was hard calling the thing *Dad*, but he managed.

The yellow thing sat across from him in silence with its unblinking stare and frozen grin, an untouched pizza slice on a plate in front of it beside an untouched glass of punch.

*Could it even eat?* Oswald wondered. Did it need to? What was it anyway? At first he thought it was a guy in a suit, but now he wasn't so sure. Was it some kind of highly sophisticated animatronic animal, or a real, flesh-and-blood giant bunny? He didn't know which possibility was the most disturbing.

With great effort, he finished his pizza slice and glass of punch, then said, "Thanks for dinner, Dad. I'm going to get a glass of milk and go do my homework now."

The yellow thing just sat there.

Oswald went to the refrigerator. He checked to make sure the yellow thing wasn't watching and poured some milk into a bowl. Once he was in his room, he didn't close and lock the door because he wouldn't if he were home with Dad. Normal. Normal so as not to arouse suspicion.

He slid the bowl of milk under his bed where Jinx was still hiding. "It's going to be okay, girl," he whispered.

He hoped he was right.

He sat on his bed and in a few minutes heard Jinx lapping the milk. He knew from past experience that even when terrified, she couldn't turn down dairy products. He made a halfhearted attempt at his homework, but he couldn't concentrate. All he could think about was his dad. The yellow thing had dragged his dad into the pit and under the surface. Did this mean his dad was at Freddy Fazbear's circa 1985, wandering around an arcade of games he had played as a kid? That was the most likely explanation, unless the yellow thing had killed—

No. He couldn't let himself think that. His dad was alive. He had to be. The only way to know was to go back into the pit.

But first he was going to have to get out of the house without the yellow thing noticing.

Oswald waited until dark, then waited some more. Finally, he grabbed his shoes and tiptoed out of his room and into the hall in his sock feet. The door to his parents' bedroom was open. He sneaked a glance inside as he crept past. The yellow thing was lying on its back on his parents' bed. It appeared to be staring at the ceiling.

Or maybe it wasn't staring. Maybe it was asleep. It was hard to tell since its eyes didn't close. Did it even need to sleep?

Holding his breath, he passed his parents' room and tiptoed into the kitchen. If the yellow thing caught him, he could always say he was just getting a drink of water. The kitchen was the best escape route. The door there was less squeaky than the front door.

He slipped into his shoes and pulled the door open slowly, inch by inch. When it was open just wide enough, he slipped through and shut it softly behind him.

Then he ran. He ran through his neighborhood and past neighbors walking their dogs and kids riding bicycles. Some people looked at Oswald strangely, and he couldn't figure out why. People ran in this neighborhood all the time.

But then he realized he wasn't running like he was doing it for exercise. He was running like something was chasing him. And it might be.

It was a long way to Jeff's Pizza on foot, and Oswald knew he couldn't keep up this pace all the way there. He slowed to a walk after he was out of his neighborhood and chose to walk side streets instead of the more direct route so he'd be harder to follow.

He was afraid Jeff's Pizza might be closed by the time he reached it, but when he arrived, hot and out of breath, the lighted OPEN sign was still on. Inside, Jeff was at the counter, watching a ball game on TV, but otherwise the place was empty.

"You know we just serve whole pizzas at night. No slices," Jeff said in his usual monotone. As always, he looked exhausted.

"Yeah, I just stopped by to get a soda to go," Oswald said, his gaze roaming to the roped-off ball pit.

Jeff looked a little puzzled, but finally said, "Okay, let me get a pie out of the oven, then I'll get it for you. Orange, right?"

"Right. Thanks."

As soon as Jeff disappeared into the kitchen, Oswald ran to the back corner and dove into the pit.

The familiar musty smell filled his nose as he sank beneath the surface. He sat on the pit's floor. He counted to one hundred as he always did, even though he wasn't sure it served any purpose in getting him to make the jump to Freddy Fazbear's in 1985. He shifted on the pit's floor and felt something solid press against his lower back.

A shoe. It felt like the sole of a shoe. He scooted around and grabbed it. It was a boot, a steel-toed work boot like his dad used to wear to work at the mill and now wore to his job at the Snack Space. He moved his hand up a little. An ankle! An ankle in the kind of thick boot sock his dad liked. He crawled farther across the floor of the pit. The face. He had to feel the face. If it was some giant furry head like the yellow thing's, he might never stop screaming. But he had to find out.

His hand found a shoulder. He reached to the chest and felt the cheap fabric of a white undershirt. He was shaking as he reached higher. He felt an unmistakably human face. Skin and stubble. A man's face. Was it Dad, and was he—

He had to be alive. He had to be.

Oswald had seen shows where people who had been in emergency situations suddenly developed amazing strength and found themselves able to lift the front end of a car or tractor. This was the kind of strength Oswald needed to find. His dad wasn't a big man, but he was still a man and weighed at least twice as much as his son. He had to move his dad if he was going to save him.

If this even was his dad. If this wasn't some kind of cruel hoax set up by the yellow thing to trap him. Oswald couldn't let himself think these thoughts, not if he was going to do what he had to do.

He got behind the person, grabbed under his armpits, and pulled. Nothing happened. *Dead weight,* Oswald thought. *No, not dead, please . . . not dead.*

He pulled again, this time with more force, making a noise that was somewhere between a grunt and a roar. This time, the body moved, and Oswald pulled again, standing up and getting the person's head and shoulders above the surface. It was his dad, pale and unconscious, but breathing, definitely breathing, and around them, not Freddy Fazbear's in 1985, but the normal, present-day weirdness of Jeff's Pizza.

How could Oswald get him out? He could call Mom.

As a nurse, she would know what to do. But what if she thought he was crazy or lying? He felt like the Boy Who Cried Wolf. Or the Boy Who Cried Rabbit.

He felt it before he saw it. The presence behind him, the awareness of something in his personal space. Before he could turn around, a pair of furry yellow arms locked around him in a fearsome embrace.

He got his right arm free enough to jab his elbow into the yellow thing's midsection. He got loose, but the thing was blocking the exit to the pit. He couldn't get out of the pit by himself, let alone with his poor, passed-out dad.

Acting more than thinking, Oswald charged at the rabbit with his head down. If he could just throw it off balance or knock it under the surface, maybe he could make it end up in 1985 Freddy Fazbear's and buy Oswald and his dad some time to escape.

He head-butted the yellow thing and knocked it into the ropes and netting that surrounded the ball pit. It stumbled a little, righted itself, and then, arms outstretched, lunged toward Oswald. It pushed Oswald against the wall of the pit. Its eyes dead as always, it unhinged its jaws to reveal double rows of fangs as sharp as scimitars. Mouth open freakishly wide, it lunged for Oswald's throat, but he blocked it with his arm.

Pain pierced Oswald's forearm as the yellow thing sank its fangs into his skin.

Oswald used his good arm to punch the rabbit hard in the face before the fangs pierced too deeply. Fangs. What kind of crazy rabbit had fangs?

The thing's jaws released their grip, but there was no time to survey the damage because the thing was lurching toward Oswald's dad, its jaws wide open, like a snake about to swallow its unsuspecting prey.

Its fangs were red with Oswald's blood.

Oswald elbowed the yellow thing aside and moved between it and his still-unconscious father. "You leave . . . my dad . . . ALONE!" he yelled, then used the netting to bounce off and clamber onto the yellow thing's back. He hit its head with his fists, scratched at its eyes, which didn't feel like a living creature's eyes. The rabbit stumbled back into the netting and ropes, then grabbed Oswald's arms and slung him hard off its shoulders and into the pit.

Oswald fell headfirst under the surface, grateful that the bottom of the pit was soft. His arm was throbbing, his whole body was exhausted, but he had to get up. He had to save his dad. Like those ancient Greek heroes Gabrielle had told him about, he had to be brave and face the monster.

Oswald rose unsteadily to his feet.

Somehow, when it shook Oswald off, the yellow thing must have gotten tangled in the ropes and netting that lined the ball pit. A rope was looped around its neck, and it grasped the rope with its big paws, trying to get free. Oswald couldn't understand why it was failing to free itself until he saw that the yellow thing's feet weren't touching the floor of the pit. The yellow thing was suspended from the rope, which was tied securely to a metal rod at the top of the ball pit.

The rabbit had hanged itself. Its mouth was opening and closing like it was gasping for breath, but no sound came out. Its paws clawed desperately at the ropes. Its stare, still terrifying in its blankness, was aimed in Oswald's direction, as if it were asking him for help.

Oswald certainly wasn't going to rescue it.

After a few more seconds of struggling, the yellow thing was still. Oswald blinked. Hanging from the rope was nothing but a dirty, empty yellow rabbit costume.

His dad's eyes opened. Oswald rushed to his side.

"I don't understand why I'm here," Dad said. His face was pale and unshaven, his eyes puffy with dark half-moons under them. "What happened?"

Oswald debated what to say: *You were attacked and left for dead by a giant evil rabbit who tried to replace you, and I was the only person who could see it wasn't you. Even Mom thought it was you.*

No. It sounded too crazy, and Oswald didn't relish the idea of spending years in therapy saying, *But the evil rabbit WAS real.*

Jinx was the only other member of the family who knew the truth, and being a cat, she wasn't going to say anything in his defense.

Besides, his dad had already suffered enough.

Oswald knew it was wrong to lie. He also knew that lying was not a skill he had. When he tried, he always got all nervous and sweaty and said "uh" a lot. But in this situation, a lie might be the only way forward. He took a deep breath.

"So, uh . . . I hid in the ball pit to play a prank on you, which I shouldn't have done. You came to look for me, and I guess you must've hit your head and lost consciousness." Oswald took a deep breath. "I'm sorry, Dad. I didn't mean for things to get so out of hand."

This part, at least, was the truth.

"I accept your apology, son," Dad said. He didn't sound mad, just tired. "But you're right—you shouldn't have done it. And Jeff really should get rid of this ball pit before he has a lawsuit on his hands."

"Definitely," Oswald said. He knew he would never set foot in the pit again. He would miss Chip and Mike, but he needed to make some friends in his own time. His mind flashed to the girl on the bench at recess. Gabrielle. She seemed nice. Smart, too. They had had a good talk.

Oswald reached for his dad's hand. "Let me help you stand up."

# INTO THE PIT

With Oswald steadying him, Dad rose to his feet and let his son lead him to the exit of the ball pit. He paused to look up at the hanging yellow costume. "What is that creepy thing?"

"I have no idea," said Oswald.

This, too, was the truth.

They climbed out of the pit and walked through Jeff's Pizza. Jeff was wiping the counter, still watching the ball game on the restaurant's TV. Had he not seen or heard anything?

Still holding Oswald's hand—when was the last time he and his dad had held hands?—Dad lifted his son's arm and looked at it. "You're bleeding."

"Yeah," Oswald said, "I must've scraped my arm when I was trying to pull you out of the pit."

His dad shook his head. "Like I said, that thing is a public safety issue. Just sticking up a sign saying KEEP OUT isn't enough." He let go of Oswald's arm. "We'll get your arm cleaned up at the house, and then your mom can dress the wound once she gets home from work."

Oswald wondered what his mom would say when she saw the fang marks.

As they approached the front door, Oswald said, "Dad, I know I can be a pain sometimes, but I really do love you, you know."

Dad looked at him with an expression that seemed both

pleased and surprised. "Same here, kiddo." He ruffled Oswald's hair. "But you do have terrible taste in science-fiction movies."

"Oh, yeah?" Oswald said, smiling. "Well, you have terrible taste in music. And you like boring ice cream."

Together, they opened the door into the fresh night air.

Behind them, Jeff called, "Hey, kid! You forgot your soda!"

# TO BE BEAUTIFUL

*Flat* and *fat*. Those were the two words that Sarah thought of when she looked in the mirror. Which she did a lot.

How could somebody with such a curved belly be as flat as an ironing board everywhere else? Other girls could describe their shapes as being like an hourglass or a pear. Sarah was shaped like a potato. Looking at her bulbous nose, her prominent ears, and how all her parts seemed stuck onto her body at random, she was reminded of the Mrs. Mix-and-Match doll she had as a kid. The one with different eyes, ears, noses, mouths, and other body parts you could stick on her to make her look as hilarious as you wanted. And so that was the nickname she came up with for herself: Mrs. Mix-and-Match.

But at least Mrs. Mix-and-Match had Mr. Mix-and-

Match. Unlike the girls at school whom she called the Beautifuls, Sarah didn't have a boyfriend or any prospect of one. Sure, there was one boy she looked at, dreamed of, but she knew he wasn't looking at or dreaming of her. She guessed that she, like Mrs. Mix-and-Match in her single days, would just have to wait around until some equally unfortunate-looking guy came along.

But in the meantime, she needed to finish getting ready for school.

Still looking at her worst enemy, the mirror, she applied some mascara and pink-tinted lip balm. For her birthday, her mom had finally given her permission to wear a little light makeup. She gave her dull, mousy brown hair a thorough brushing. She sighed. It was as good as it was going to get. And it wasn't good.

The walls of Sarah's room were decorated with photos of models and pop stars she had cut out of magazines. Their eyes were smoky, their lips full, their legs long. They were slender, curvy and confident, young but womanly, and their perfect bodies were wearing clothes Sarah couldn't even dream of affording. Sometimes when she was getting ready in the morning, she felt as if these goddesses of beauty were looking at her with disappointment. *Oh,* they seemed to say, *is THAT what you're wearing?* Or, *No hope of a modeling career for you, sweetheart.* Still, she liked having the goddesses there. If she couldn't see beauty when she looked in the mirror, at least she could see it when she looked at the walls.

In the kitchen, her mom was dressed for work in a long floral print dress, her salt-and-pepper hair long and loose down her back. Her mom never wore makeup or did anything special with her hair, and she had a tendency to put on weight around her hips. Still, Sarah had to admit that her mom had a natural prettiness she herself lacked. *Maybe it skips a generation,* Sarah thought.

"Hey, cupcake," Mom said. "I picked up some bagels. I got that kind you like with all the seeds. You want me to pop one in the toaster for you?"

"No, I'll just have a yogurt," Sarah said, though her mouth watered at the thought of a toasty Everything bagel slathered in cream cheese. "I don't need all those carbs."

Mom rolled her eyes. "Sarah, those little yogurt cups you live on have just ninety calories in them. It's a wonder you don't pass out from hunger in school." She took a big bite of the bagel she had fixed for herself. She had put the top and bottom together sandwich-style, and cream cheese squished out when she chomped it. "Besides," Mom said, her mouth full, "you're much too young to be worried about carbs."

*And you're much too old* not *to be worried about them,* Sarah wanted to say, but she stopped herself. Instead, she said, "A yogurt and a bottle of water will be plenty to hold me over until lunchtime."

"Suit yourself," Mom said. "But I'm telling you, this bagel is delicious."

Unlike most mornings, Sarah actually made it to the school bus in time, so she didn't have to walk. She sat by herself and watched YouTube makeup tutorials on her phone. Maybe on her next birthday Mom would let her wear more than mascara and BB cream and tinted lip balm. She could get what she needed to do some real contouring, to make her cheekbones look more pronounced and her nose less bulbous. Getting her brows done professionally would also really help. Right now she and her tweezers were fighting a daily battle against a unibrow.

Before first period, as she got her science book out of her locker, she saw them. They strutted down the hall like supermodels doing a runway show, and everybody—*everybody*—stopped what they were doing to watch them. Lydia, Jillian, Tabitha, and Emma. They were cheerleaders. They were royalty. They were stars. They were who every girl in the school wanted to be and who every boy in the school wanted to be with.

They were the Beautifuls.

Each girl had her own particular brand of beauty. Lydia had blonde hair and blue eyes and a rosy complexion, while Jillian had fiery red hair and catlike green eyes. Tabitha was dark with chocolate-brown eyes and lustrous black hair, and Emma had chestnut hair and enormous doe-like brown eyes. All the girls had long hair—the better to flip luxuriously over their shoulders—and were slender but with enough curves to fill out their clothes in the bust and the hips.

And their clothes!

Their clothes were as beautiful as they were, all bought at high-end stores in big cities they visited on their vacations. Today they were all wearing black and white—a short black dress with a white collar and cuffs for Lydia, a white shirt with a black-and-white polka-dot miniskirt for Jillian, a black-and-white striped—

"What are they, penguins?" A voice cut off Sarah's admiring thoughts.

"Huh?" Sarah turned to see Abby, her best friend since kindergarten, standing beside her. She was wearing some kind of hideous poncho and a long, loose floral-print skirt. She looked like she should be running a fortune-telling booth at the school carnival.

"I said they look like penguins," Abby said. "Let's hope there aren't any hungry seals around." She made a loud barking sound, then laughed.

"You're crazy," Sarah said. "I think they look perfect."

"You always do," Abby said. She was hugging her social studies book against her chest. "And I have a theory about why."

"You have a theory about everything," Sarah said. It was true. Abby wanted to be a scientist, and all those theories would probably come in handy one day when she was working on her PhD.

"You know how we used to play Barbies when we were little?" Abby asked.

When they were little, Sarah and Abby had each had pink carrying cases filled with Barbies and their various clothes and accessories. They had taken turns carrying their cases to each other's houses and had played for hours, stopping only for juice box and graham cracker breaks. Life had been so easy back then.

"Yeah," Sarah said. It was funny. Abby hadn't changed much since those days. She still wore her hair in the same braids, still wore gold wire-framed glasses. The braces on her teeth and a few inches of height were the only differences. Still, when Sarah looked at Abby, she could at least see that the opportunity for beauty was there. Abby had a flawless coffee-with-cream complexion and startling hazel eyes behind those glasses of hers. She took dance classes after school and had a graceful, slender body, even if she hid it under hideous ponchos and other baggy clothes. Sarah had no beauty, and it tormented her. Abby had beauty, but didn't care about it enough to notice.

"My theory," Abby said, getting animated the way she did when she was lecturing, "is that you used to love to play with Barbies, but now that you're too old for them you need a Barbie substitute. Those empty-headed fashionistas are your Barbie substitute. That's why you want to play with them."

*Play?* Sometimes it was like Abby was still a little kid.

"I don't want to play with them," Sarah said, though she wasn't sure this was exactly true. "I'm too old to want to play with anybody. I just . . . admire them, is all."

Abby rolled her eyes. "What is there to admire? The fact that they can match their eye shadows to their outfits? If you'll excuse me, I think I'll go on admiring Marie Curie and Rosa Parks."

Sarah smiled. Abby had always been such a nerd. A lovable

nerd, but still, a nerd. "Well, you've never had much interest in fashion. I remember how you used to treat your Barbies."

Abby grinned back. "Well, there was the one I shaved bald. And then there was the one with the hair I colored green with a Magic Marker so she looked like some kind of crazy supervillain." She wiggled her eyebrows. "Now if those teen queens would let me play with them that way, I might be interested."

Sarah laughed. "You're the one who's a supervillain."

"Nope," Abby said, "just a smart aleck. Which is why I'm way more fun than those cheerleaders." Abby gave a little wave and then hurried off to class.

At lunch Sarah sat across from Abby. It was Friday, which was pizza day, and on Abby's tray was one of the school's rectangular pizza slices, a cup of fruit cocktail, and a carton of milk. School pizza wasn't the best, but it was still pizza so it was pretty good. Too many carbs, though. Sarah had hit the salad bar instead and had gotten a green salad with low-fat vinaigrette dressing. She liked ranch a lot better than vinaigrette, but ranch added too many calories.

The other kids at the table were the nerds who hurried through their lunch so they could play card games until the bell rang. Sarah knew the Beautifuls called it the loser table.

Sarah stabbed at her lettuce with her dull plastic fork. "What would you do," she asked Abby, "if you had a million dollars?"

Abby grinned. "Oh, that's easy. First I'd—"

"Wait," Sarah said because she knew the kind of thing Abby was going to say. "You're not allowed to say you'd give it to the Humane Society or the homeless or whatever. The money's just to spend on yourself."

Abby smiled. "And since it's imaginary money, I don't have to feel guilty."

"That's right," Sarah said, crunching on a baby carrot.

"Okay." Abby took a bite of pizza and chewed thoughtfully. "Well, in that case, I'd use it to travel. Paris first, I think, with my mom and dad and brother. We'd stay in a fancy hotel and go to the Eiffel Tower and the Louvre and eat at the best restaurants and stuff ourselves with pastries and drink coffee at fancy cafés and people-watch. What would you do?"

Sarah pushed her salad around on her plate. "Well, I'd definitely get my teeth professionally whitened, and I'd go to one of those high-end salons and get my hair cut and colored. Blonde, but a realistic-looking blonde. I'd get skin treatments and a makeover with really good makeup, not the cheap drugstore kind. And I'd get a nose job. There are other cosmetic procedures I'd like to have, but I don't think they'll do them on a kid."

"And they shouldn't!" Abby said. She looked shocked, like Sarah had said something really bad. "Seriously, you'd put yourself through all that pain and suffering just to change the way you *look*? I had my tonsils taken out, and it was horrible. I'll never have another operation if I can help it." She looked at Sarah intensely. "What's wrong with your nose anyway?"

Sarah put her hand to her nose. "Isn't it obvious? It's huge."

Abby laughed. "No, it's not. It's just a regular nose. A nice nose. And when you think about it, does anybody really have a beautiful nose? Noses are kind of weird. I actually like animal noses better than people noses. My dog has a really cute nose."

Sarah shot a glance over to the Beautifuls' table. All of them had perfect tiny noses, adorable little buttons. Not a potato nose in the bunch.

Abby looked over to the table where Sarah was looking. "Oh, the Penguins again? Okay, so the thing about penguins is they may be cute, but they all look alike. You're a person, and you should look like an individual."

"Yeah, an ugly individual," Sarah said, pushing away her salad plate.

"No, a nice-looking individual who worries too much about her appearance." Abby reached out and touched Sarah's forearm. "You've changed a lot in the past couple years, Sarah. We used to talk about books and movies and music. Now all you want to talk about is how you don't like the way you look and about all the clothes and hairstyles and makeup you wish you could afford. And instead of having pictures on your wall of cute baby animals like you used to, you've got pictures of all those skinny models. I liked the baby animals a lot better."

Sarah felt anger rising like bile in her throat. How dare Abby judge her? Friends were supposed to be the people who didn't judge you. She stood up. "You're right, Abby," she said, loud enough that the other people at the table turned to look at her. "I have changed. I've grown up, and you haven't. I think about adult things, and you still buy stickers and watch cartoons and draw horses!"

Sarah was so angry that she marched off and left her tray on the table for somebody else to clean up.

By the time school was over, Sarah had a plan. She wasn't going to sit at the loser table anymore because she wasn't going to be a loser. She was going to be as popular and as pretty as she possibly could be.

It was amazing how quickly her plan fell into place. As soon as she was home, she dug in her dresser drawer where she kept her money. She had twenty dollars of birthday money from her grandma and ten left from her allowance. It was enough.

The beauty supply store was just about a fifteen-minute walk from her house. She could get there and back and do what she needed to do before her mom got home at six.

The store was brightly lit, with row after row of beauty

products: brushes and curling irons, hair dryers, nail polish, and makeup. She headed for the aisle labeled HAIR COLOR. She didn't have to have a million dollars to become a blonde. She could do it for around ten bucks and just look like a million. She selected a box marked PURE PLATINUM, decorated with a picture of a smiling model with long, luminous, white-gold hair. Beautiful.

The woman at the checkout counter had obviously dyed, bright red hair and false eyelashes that made her resemble a giraffe. "Now if you want your hair to look like the picture, you'll have to bleach it first," she said.

"Bleach it . . . how?" Sarah asked. Her mom used bleach and water to clean the floors sometimes. Surely this wasn't the same thing.

"You'll wanna get the peroxide that's back on aisle two," the cashier said.

When Sarah returned with the plastic bottle, the woman looked at her with narrowed eyes. "Does your mama know you're about to color your hair, hon?"

"Oh, sure," Sarah said, not making eye contact. "She doesn't mind." She didn't know if her mom would mind or not. She guessed she would find out.

"Well, that's good, then," she said, ringing up Sarah's purchases. "Maybe she can help you. Make sure you get the color on good and even."

At home, Sarah locked herself in the bathroom and

read the directions from the box of hair color. They seemed simple enough. She put on the plastic gloves that came with the hair dye kit, draped a towel around her shoulders, and worked the peroxide into her hair. She wasn't sure how long to leave the peroxide on, so she sat on the edge of the bathtub and played a few games on her phone and watched some YouTube makeup tutorials.

First her scalp started to itch. Then it started to burn. It burned as if someone had thrown a handful of lit matches into her hair. She quickly typed into her phone, "how long to leave peroxide in hair."

The answer that appeared was "no longer than 30 minutes."

How long had she left it in? She jumped to her feet, grabbed the detachable showerhead, turned the water on cold, leaned her head over the tub, and started spraying. The frigid water soothed her fiery scalp.

When she looked in the bathroom mirror, her hair was stark white, like she had become an old woman way before her time. The bathroom stank of bleach, making her nose run and her eyes water. She cracked the window and opened the bottle of hair color.

It was time to complete her transformation.

She shook up the hair color ingredients in a squeeze bottle and squirted the mixture all over her hair and massaged it in. She set the alarm on her phone to go off in twenty-five minutes and settled in to wait. By the time her mom got home, Sarah was going to look like a whole new person.

She played happily on her phone until the alarm buzzed, then rinsed off again with the detachable showerhead. She didn't bother with the conditioner that came with the hair color kit because she was too anxious to see the results. She toweled off her hair and stepped over to the mirror to see the new her.

She screamed.

She screamed so loud that the neighbor's dog started barking. Her hair was not platinum blonde but sewage green. She thought of Abby when they were little, coloring her Barbie's hair with a green Magic Marker. Now she *was* that Barbie.

How? How could she do something to make herself pretty and end up even uglier than before? Why was life so unfair? She ran to her room, flung herself onto her bed, and cried. She must have cried herself into a miserable sleep because the next thing she knew, her mom was sitting on the edge of the bed saying, "What happened here?"

Sarah looked up. She could see the shock in her mom's eyes. "I—I was trying to color my hair," Sarah sobbed. "I wanted to be blonde, but I'm—I'm . . ."

"You're green. I can see that," Mom said. "Well, I would say there would be consequences from you coloring your hair without my permission, but I think you're already experiencing some of those. You are going to clean up the bathroom, though. But for right now, we need to see what we can do to make you look less like . . . a Martian." She touched Sarah's hair. "Oof! It feels like straw. Listen, put on your shoes. The hair salon at the mall should still be open. Maybe they can fix this."

Sarah put on her shoes and stuffed her moss-colored tresses under a baseball cap. When they got to the salon and Sarah yanked off the cap, the stylist gasped. "Well, it's a good thing you called nine one one. This is definitely a hair emergency."

An hour and a half later, Sarah was back to having brown hair, now a few inches shorter because the stylist had to cut off the damaged ends.

"Well," Mom said, once they were in the car on the way home, "that was a big chunk of my paycheck. I probably should've just let you go to school with green hair. It would've served you right."

Sarah returned to school not in a blaze of platinum-blonde glory but as her usual mousy-brown self. Still, when lunchtime rolled around, she resolved that, even without blonde hair, she wasn't going to sit at the loser table. She served herself from the salad bar, then walked right past where Abby was sitting. She didn't need Abby to criticize her today.

A knot formed in her stomach as she approached the Beautifuls' table. They must have decided today was Jeans Day because they were all wearing cute skinny jeans with fitted jewel-colored tops and matching slip-on canvas shoes.

Sarah sat down at the opposite end of the table, far enough away that she didn't seem to be intruding but close enough that they could include her if they wanted.

She waited a few minutes, expecting one of them to tell her to go away, but nobody did. She was relieved and hopeful, but then she realized that none of them even seemed to see her. They just kept right on with their conversation like she was invisible.

"She did not say that!"

"Oh, yes, she did!"

"No!"

"Yes!"

"And then what did he say?"

Sarah pushed her salad around on her plate and tried to follow the conversation, but she had no idea who they were talking about and she certainly wasn't going to ask them. Probably they wouldn't even hear her if she said something. If they couldn't see her, they probably couldn't hear her, either. She felt like a ghost.

She picked up her tray and headed toward the trash can, desperate to get out of the cafeteria—desperate to get out of the whole school, really. But there was still seventh and eighth periods to suffer through, boring social studies and stupid math. Lost in her suffering, she bumped right into a tall boy, dumping the remains of her salad on his crisp white shirt.

She looked up into the ocean-blue eyes of Mason Blair, the most perfect guy in school, the guy she always hoped might notice her.

"Hey, watch where you're going," he said, picking a cucumber slice off his expensive designer shirt. The vinaigrette-covered vegetable had left a perfect oily circle in the middle of his chest.

"Sorry!" she squeaked, then threw the rest of her salad—what Mason wasn't wearing—into the trash and half ran out of the cafeteria.

What a nightmare. She had wanted Mason to notice her, but not this way. Not as the ugly, clumsy girl with fried, frizzy brown hair who gave a new meaning to the words *tossed salad*. Why did everything have to go wrong for her? The Beautifuls never did anything stupid or clumsy, never humiliated themselves in front of a cute boy. Their beauty was like a suit of armor that protected them from life's pain and embarrassment.

When the school day finally dragged to an end, Sarah decided to walk home instead of taking the bus. Given how her day had been, she didn't feel like she should take the risk of being with a big group of kids again. It would just be inviting disaster.

She walked alone, telling herself she might as well get used to solitude. She was always going to be alone. She passed the Brown Cow, the ice-cream stand where the Beautifuls went with their boyfriends after school, laughing as they sat together at picnic tables, sharing milk shakes or sundaes. And of course the Beautifuls could scarf all the ice cream they wanted and not gain an ounce. Life was so unfair.

To get to her house, Sarah had to walk past the wrecking yard. It was an ugly expanse of dirt filled with the destroyed corpses of cars. There were smashed-in pickup trucks, squashed SUVs, and vehicles that had been reduced to nothing more than rusted heaps of junk. She was sure that none of the Beautifuls had to pass a place so hideous on their way home.

Even though the junkyard was horrible—or maybe *because* it was so horrible—she couldn't help looking at it when she passed by. She was like a passing driver gawking at an accident on the side of the road.

The car nearest the fence definitely fit into the "heap of junk" category. It was one of those big, old sedans that only very elderly people still drove, the kind of car Sarah's mom called a land yacht. This yacht had seen better days. It had once been light blue, but now it was mostly rusty orange-brown. In some places the rust had eaten all the way through the metal, and the car's body was so battered it looked like it had been attacked by an angry mob wielding baseball bats.

Then she saw the arm.

A thin, delicate arm was sticking out of the trunk of the car, its little white hand with fingers outstretched as if waving hello. Or waving for help, like someone who was drowning.

Sarah burned with curiosity. What was the hand attached to?

The gate was unlocked. Nobody seemed to be watching. After looking around to make sure no one was nearby, she stepped inside the wrecking yard.

She approached the old sedan and touched the arm, then the hand. It was metal, from the feel of it. She found the handle on the trunk and pulled it, but the lever wouldn't budge. The car was so dented and battered that the trunk wouldn't open and close properly anymore.

Sarah thought of the story a teacher had read to her class once in elementary school about King Arthur pulling a sword from a stone when nobody else could. Could she pull this doll—or whatever it was—from this wrecked vehicle? She looked around until she found a strong, flat piece of metal that could maybe work as a substitute crowbar.

Sarah braced her foot against the car's crumpled bumper, slid the metal inside the trunk door, and pried upward. The first time she tried, it didn't give at all, but the second time, it flipped open and threw her off balance. She fell backward and landed on her butt in the dirt. She stood up to inspect the owner of the hand she had seen sticking out of the trunk.

Was it a discarded doll, outgrown by some little girl and tossed in the trash to end up in the dump? The thought made Sarah sad.

Sarah pulled the doll from the trunk and stood it up on its feet, though once she looked at it, she wasn't sure *doll* was the right word to describe it. It was a few inches taller than Sarah herself, and it was jointed so that its limbs and waist looked movable. Was it some kind of marionette? A robot?

Whatever it was, it was beautiful. It had wide, green, long-lashed eyes, pink Cupid's bow lips, and pink circles on its cheeks. Its face was painted like a clown's, but a pretty clown. Its red hair was pulled up into twin pigtails on top of its head, and its body was sleek and silver, with a long neck, a tiny waist, and a rounded bust and hips. Its legs and arms were long, slender, and elegant. It looked like a robotic version of the gorgeous supermodels whose pictures hung on the walls of Sarah's room.

Where had it come from? And why would someone want to get rid of such a beautiful, perfect object?

Well, if whoever put this thing in the dump didn't want it, then Sarah did. She picked up the girl-shaped robot and found it surprisingly light. She carried it sideways, her arm around its delicate waist.

At home, in her room, Sarah set the girl robot down on the floor. It was a little tarnished and dusty, as if it had been in the trash heap for a while. Sarah went to the kitchen and got a rag and a bottle of cleaner that was supposed to be safe for metal surfaces. She sprayed and wiped the front of the robot, inch by inch, from head to toe. The shininess made it even more beautiful. As Sarah got behind the robot to clean the other side, she noticed an on-off switch at the small of its back. After she finished wiping it down, she turned the switch position to On.

Nothing happened. Sarah turned away, slightly disappointed. The robot was still cool to have, though, even if it didn't do anything.

But then a rattling sound made Sarah turn back around. The robot was shaking all over, like it was either going to rev up or break down entirely. Then it went still.

Sarah resigned herself once more to the idea that the robot wasn't going to do anything.

Until it did.

The robot's waist pivoted, making its upper body move.

It slowly raised its arms and then put them down. Its head turned to face Sarah, seeming to look at her with its big green eyes.

"Hello, friend," it said, in a slightly metallic-sounding version of a young girl's voice. "My name is Eleanor."

Sarah knew the thing couldn't be talking to her personally, but it felt like it was. "Hi," she whispered, feeling a little silly for entering into a conversation with an inanimate object. "I'm Sarah."

"Nice to meet you, Sarah," the girl robot said.

Whoa. How had it said her name back to her? *It must have some pretty sophisticated built-in computer or something,* Sarah thought. It was the kind of thing her brother might know about; he was in college majoring in computer science.

The robot took a few surprisingly smooth steps toward Sarah. "Thank you for rescuing me and cleaning me up, Sarah," Eleanor the robot said. "I feel as good as new." She gave a pretty, feminine twirl, her short skirt billowing.

Sarah's mouth was hanging open. Was this thing capable of actual conversation, of actual *thought*? "Um . . . you're welcome?" she said.

"Now," Eleanor said, placing her cold, hard little hand on Sarah's cheek. "You tell me what I can do for you, Sarah."

Sarah stared at the robot's blankly pretty face. "What do you mean?"

"You did something nice for me. Now I must do

something nice for *you*." Eleanor cocked her head like an adorable puppy. "What do you want, Sarah? I want to make your wishes come true."

"Uh, nothing, really," Sarah said. It wasn't the truth, but really, how could this robot make her wishes come true?

"Everybody wants something," Eleanor said, brushing Sarah's hair away from her face. "What do you want, Sarah?"

Sarah took a deep breath. She looked at the images of models and actresses and pop stars on her walls. She might as well say it. Eleanor was a robot; she wouldn't judge her. "I want . . . ," she whispered, feeling embarrassed. "I want . . . to be beautiful."

Eleanor clapped her hands. "To be beautiful! What a wonderful wish! But it is a large wish, Sarah, and I am petite. Give me twenty-four hours, and I will have a plan to start making this wish come true."

"Okay, sure," Sarah said. But she didn't believe for one minute that this robot had the ability to transform her looks. She couldn't even quite believe that she was having a real conversation with it.

When Sarah woke up the next morning, Eleanor was standing in the corner as still and lifeless as the other decorative objects in Sarah's room, no more alive than the stuffed Freddy Fazbear she'd had on her bed since she was six. Maybe the conversation with Eleanor had just been a particularly vivid dream.

That afternoon, when Sarah got home from school, Eleanor pivoted her waist, raised and lowered her arms, and moved smoothly over to Sarah. "I made you something, Sarah," she said. Eleanor put her hands behind her back and produced a necklace. It was a chunky silver chain with a large, cartoonish silver heart pendant dangling from it. It was unusual. Pretty.

"You made this for me?" Sarah said.

"I did," Eleanor said. "I want you to make me a promise. I want you to put this necklace on and never, ever take it off. Do you promise you'll keep it on, always?"

"I promise," Sarah said. "Thank you for making it for me. It's beautiful."

"And you will be beautiful, too," Eleanor said. "Since your wish is so big, Sarah, I can only grant it a little at a time. But if you wear this necklace and keep it on, each morning when you wake up you'll be a little more beautiful than the day before." Eleanor held out the necklace, and Sarah took it.

"Okay, thanks," Sarah said, not believing Eleanor for a minute. But she put on the necklace anyway because it was pretty.

"It looks good on you," Eleanor said. "Now for the

necklace to work, you have to let me sing you to sleep."

"Like, now?" Sarah asked.

Eleanor nodded.

"It's early, though. Mom isn't even home from work yet—"

"For the necklace to work, you have to let me sing you to sleep," Eleanor repeated.

"Well, I guess I could take a little nap," Sarah said, not entirely sure that she wasn't already asleep and dreaming.

"Get into bed," Eleanor said, moving in her smooth stroll to the side of Sarah's bed. Even though she was a robot, everything about Eleanor was so feminine and lovely.

Sarah pulled back the covers and got into bed. Eleanor sat on the edge of the bed and stroked Sarah's hair with her cold little hand. She sang,

*Go to sleep, go to sleep,*
*Go to sleep, my sweet Sarah,*
*When you wake, when you wake,*
*All your dreams will come true.*

Before Eleanor sang the last note, Sarah was asleep.

Sarah was usually groggy and grumpy in the morning, but this morning she woke up feeling great. Eleanor, she noticed, was standing still in the corner of the room in her inanimate object pose. Somehow Eleanor being there made Sarah feel safe, as if Eleanor were standing guard.

Maybe Eleanor was just an inanimate object, Sarah thought as she sat up in bed. But then she reached up and felt the silver heart pendant hanging just below her throat. If the necklace was real, the talk she had with Eleanor must be real, too. As she moved her hand away from the necklace, she noticed something else.

Her arm. Both her arms, actually. They were slimmer and more toned somehow, and their skin, which was usually sallow, was healthy and glowing. The dry patches of skin she was prone to had disappeared, and both arms were soft and smooth to the touch. Even her usually chapped elbows were as soft as kittens' noses.

And her fingers—as she touched her arms with them, they felt different, too. She stretched out her hands to inspect them. Her once stubby fingers were long, elegant, and tapered. Her formerly short, nubby nails were now longer than her fingertips and shaped in perfect ovals. Amazingly, they were also painted a gorgeous, soft pink, each nail like a perfect rose petal.

Sarah ran to the mirror to give herself a full inspection. Same mix and match face, nose, and body, but now with a perfect pair of arms and hands. She thought of Eleanor's words from last night: "Each morning when you wake up you'll be a little more beautiful than the day before."

Sarah was definitely a little more beautiful. Was this the way it was going to work—that every morning a different part of her would be transformed?

She darted to the corner where Eleanor was standing. "I love my new arms and hands! Thank you!" she said to the unmoving robot. "So, like, am I going to wake up every morning to one new part until I'm totally transformed?"

Eleanor didn't move. Her face kept the same painted-on expression.

"Well, maybe I'll just have to wait and see, huh?" Sarah said. "Thanks again." She stood on tiptoe, kissed the robot on its cold, hard cheek, and then hurried to the kitchen for breakfast.

Her mom was sitting at the table with a cup of coffee and half a grapefruit. "Wow, I didn't even have to yell at you to get out of bed this morning," Mom said. "What's going on?"

Sarah shrugged. "I don't know. I just woke up feeling good. I slept well, I guess." She poured some cornflakes in a bowl and drenched them with milk.

"Well, you were already passed out when I got home. I thought about waking you for dinner, but you were out like a light," Mom said. She watched as Sarah shoveled in cereal. "And you're eating real food, too. Would you like the other half of this grapefruit?"

"Sure, thanks," Sarah said.

As she reached for the grapefruit, her mom grabbed her hand. "Hey, when did you let your nails grow out?"

Sarah knew she couldn't say "last night," so she said, "Over the past couple of weeks, I guess."

"Well, they look fantastic," Mom said, giving her hand a squeeze before she let it go. "Healthy, too. Have you been taking those vitamins I bought you?"

Sarah hadn't been but said yes anyway.

"Good," her mom said, smiling. "It's definitely paying off."

After breakfast, Sarah selected a pink shirt that complemented her nail color and took some extra time with her hair and makeup. At school she felt a little less invisible.

While she was in the restroom washing her hands, Jillian, one of the Beautifuls, came in. She checked her perfect face and hair in the mirror, then glanced down at Sarah's hands. "Ooh, I love that polish," she said.

Sarah was so shocked she could barely manage to say "Thanks."

Jillian flounced out of the restroom, no doubt to join her popular friends.

But she had *seen* Sarah. She had *noticed* Sarah, and she

had liked at least one thing about her.

Sarah smiled to herself for the rest of the day.

Eleanor was mostly nocturnal. When the last of the winter daylight started to fade, she pivoted her waist, moved her arms up and down, and sprang to life.

"Hello, Sarah," she said in her tinny little voice. "Are you a little more beautiful today than you were yesterday, just like I promised?"

"Yes," Sarah said. She couldn't remember ever feeling so grateful. "Thank you."

Eleanor nodded her head. "Good. And are you a little happier today than you were yesterday?"

"I am," said Sarah.

Eleanor clapped her little hands. "Good. That's what I want. To grant your wishes and make you happy."

Sarah still couldn't quite believe this all was happening. "That's really nice of you. But why?"

"I told you why. You saved me, Sarah. You pulled me out of the trash heap, cleaned me up, and brought me back to life. And so now I want to grant you wishes just like a fairy godmother. Would you like that?" Her voice, while metallic, also sounded kind.

"Yes," Sarah said. Who wouldn't like a fairy godmother?

"Good," Eleanor said. "Then never, ever take off that necklace, and let me sing you to sleep. When you wake up you'll be a little more beautiful than you are today."

Sarah hesitated. She knew her mom had thought it was weird when she came home yesterday evening and found Sarah already asleep. If Sarah fell asleep early every night, her mom would worry that she was sick or something. Plus, there was the homework issue. If she stopped doing her homework, that, too, would arouse suspicion, both at home and at school.

"I'll let you sing me to sleep," Sarah said. "But could it be in a few hours? I need to eat dinner with my mom and then do my homework."

"If you must," Eleanor said, sounding a little disappointed. "But it is necessary that you let me put you to sleep as early as possible. It's important that you get your beauty rest."

After a spaghetti dinner and an hour and a half of math and English, Sarah took a quick shower, brushed her teeth, and put on her nightgown. Then she approached Eleanor, who was standing still in her corner.

"I'm ready," Sarah said.

"Then get in bed like a good girl," Eleanor said.

Sarah climbed under the covers, and Eleanor came to the bed with her rolling gait. She sat on the edge of the bed and reached out to touch Sarah's heart-shaped pendant. "Remember to keep it on always and never, ever take it off," Eleanor said.

"I'll remember," Sarah said.

Eleanor stroked Sarah's hair with her cold little hand and sang her lullaby:

*Go to sleep, go to sleep,*
*Go to sleep, my sweet Sarah,*
*When you wake, when you wake,*
*All your dreams will come true.*

Once again, Sarah fell asleep before she knew what hit her.

She woke feeling refreshed, and when she stood up, she seemed to stand a little straighter, a little prouder, a little . . . TALLER?

She ran to the mirror and pulled up her nightgown to expose her legs.

They were magnificent. She was no longer stubby Mrs. Mix-and-Match with legless feet stuck onto her dumpy body. Her legs were long and shapely, with toned calves and dainty ankles, a model's legs. When she ran her hands over them, the skin was smooth and sleek. She looked down and noticed that the nails on her perfect, adorable toes were polished the same rosy pink as her fingernails.

Sarah usually wore jeans to school, the better to cover her stubby limbs. But today she was going to wear a dress. She ran to her closet and took out a lovely lavender dress her mom had bought her last spring. She hadn't liked the way it looked on her then, but now it showed off her long, shapely arms and legs. She slipped on some ballet flats and admired her reflection in the mirror.

She still didn't look exactly how she wanted to (that potato nose had to go, for one thing), but she was definitely making progress. She put on the little bit of makeup she was allowed to wear, brushed her hair, and went down to breakfast.

Her mom was standing at the stove, stirring eggs in a pan. "Look at you! You're a knockout!" Mom looked her up and down, smiling. "Is it picture day or something?"

"No," Sarah said, sitting down at the table and pouring herself a glass of orange juice. "I just felt like making an effort today."

"Is there somebody special you're making an effort for?" Mom asked in a teasing tone.

Sarah's mind wandered for a moment to Mason Blair, but then the image turned into her bumping into him and covering him with salad. "No, just for me, I guess."

Mom smiled. "Wow, that's really nice to hear. Hey, do you want some eggs?"

Sarah felt a sudden, ravenous hunger. "Sure," she said.

Her mom dished up scrambled eggs and toast for each of them and then sat down. "I don't know what it is," Mom said, "but for the past couple of days you've just seemed so much more mature and easy to talk to." She sipped her coffee and looked thoughtful. "Maybe you'd just been going through an awkward stage the last year or so, and you're starting to outgrow it."

Sarah smiled. "Yes, I think that may be it." *The awkward stage was my entire life before I met Eleanor,* Sarah thought.

At school, Sarah saw Abby in the hall and felt a pang of missing her. The two of them had so much history together, going back to the days of finger paint and Play-Doh. But Abby was stubborn. If Sarah waited for Abby to apologize to her, it might never happen.

She walked up to Abby at her locker. "Hey," Sarah said.

"Hey." Abby dug around in her locker and didn't make eye contact with her.

"Listen," Sarah said, "I'm sorry I said those mean things to you the other day."

Abby finally looked at her. "Hey, they weren't wrong. I do still like cartoons and stickers and horses."

"Yeah, and there's nothing wrong with that. Stickers and horses and cartoons are nice. And you're nice. And I'm sorry. Friends?" She held her hand out, and Abby laughed and hugged her instead.

When Abby pulled away from the hug, she looked Sarah up and down. "Hey, have you gotten taller or something?"

There was no way she could explain it. "No, I'm just working on having better posture."

"Well, you're definitely succeeding."

Eleanor had put Sarah to sleep with her usual sweet song the night before. This morning, still lying in bed, she looked at her body to see if she could tell which parts had gotten an upgrade. To her surprise, the parts of her that had been soft and flabby were now tight and toned, and parts that had been flat and childish were now rounded and feminine.

Sarah chose a fitted T-shirt and a denim miniskirt to wear to school. Her pitiful little training bra wouldn't hook anymore, so she made do with the sports bra she wore for gym class. It was a tight fit.

At breakfast she asked her mom, "Can we maybe go shopping this weekend?"

"Well, I get paid on Friday, so a little shopping wouldn't be out of the question," Mom said, pouring herself more coffee. "Anything in particular you're looking for?"

Sarah looked down at her chest, then grinned sheepishly.

"Oh!" her mom said, sounding startled. "Well, those certainly snuck up on me. Of course we can buy you some bras that fit." She smiled and shook her head. "I can't believe how fast you're growing up."

"Neither can I." It was true.

"It feels like it happens overnight," Mom said.

*Because it does,* Sarah thought.

At school, Sarah could feel eyes on her. Boys' eyes. For the first time, she felt noticed. She felt seen. It was dizzying. Exciting.

In the hall on the way to English, a trio of boys—cute boys—looked at her, then looked at one another and whispered something, then laughed. But it wasn't a mean or mocking laugh.

Wondering what they'd said, Sarah looked back at them and bumped right into—no, it couldn't be! Not again!—Mason Blair.

She felt her face flushing and braced herself for him to tell her to watch where she was going . . . again.

But instead, he smiled. He had really great teeth, straight and white. "We have to stop bumping into each other like this," he said.

"Actually, I think it's me bumping into you," Sarah said. "At least I wasn't carrying a salad this time."

"Yeah." His smile was dazzling. "That was really funny."

"Yeah," Sarah said, though it struck her as strange that he said the salad incident was funny now. When it had happened, he seemed annoyed.

"Well, if you're going to keep running into me, I at least need to know your name. I can't just keep calling you Salad Girl."

"I'm Sarah. But you can call me Salad Girl if you want."

"Nice to really meet you, Sarah. I'm Mason."

"I know." She could've kicked herself. So much for playing it cool.

"Okay, well, I'll see you around, Sarah the Salad Girl." He gave her one last flash of a smile.

"See you," Sarah said. She continued on her way to English, but all she could think about was that she'd just had a conversation—a real, human conversation—with Mason Blair.

Sarah sat down next to Abby in class. "Mason Blair just talked to me," Sarah whispered. "Like *talked-to-me* talked to me."

"I'm not surprised," Abby whispered back. "There's something about you lately."

"What do you mean?"

Abby crinkled her forehead the way she did when she was thinking hard. "I don't know. I can't exactly put it into words. It's like you're glowing from the inside out."

Sarah smiled. "Yeah, that is what it's like." But really, it was the changes on the outside that were making her glow inside.

In the evening, after Eleanor did her wake-up movements, Sarah threw her arms around her. It felt strange to hug something so hard and cold, and when Eleanor's arms encircled Sarah, she felt a flicker of what could have been fear, but she quickly pushed the feeling away. There was nothing to be afraid of. Eleanor was her friend.

"Eleanor," Sarah said, drawing back from the hug, "I couldn't be happier with my new body. It's perfect. Thank you so much!"

"I'm glad," Eleanor said, cocking her head. "All I want is for you to be happy, Sarah."

"Well, I'm loads happier than I was before I found you," Sarah said. "Today it was like I could feel all these people *seeing* me. And they liked what they saw. The guy I've had a crush on for months even noticed me and talked to me."

"That's wonderful," Eleanor said. "I'm glad I've been able to make all your wishes come true, Sarah."

A dark cloud suddenly passed over the brightness of Sarah's mood. "Well," she said, "not all of them." She reached up and touched her potato-y nose.

"Really?" Eleanor sounded surprised. "What is it that you still wish, Sarah?"

Sarah took a deep breath. "I love my new body," she said. "I really do. But I'm kind of what some guys call pretty from afar, but far from pretty."

Eleanor cocked her head again. "Pretty from afar? I don't understand, Sarah."

"Well, you know, guys will say, 'She looks great from far away, but don't get too close to her face.'"

"*Oh!* Far *from pretty!*" Eleanor said. "I understand now." She laughed, a metallic tinkling. "It is very amusing."

"It's not if someone's using it to describe you," Sarah said.

"I suppose it isn't," Eleanor said. She reached up and touched Sarah's cheek. "Sarah, do you really want me to change all this? Do you want a new face?"

"I do," Sarah said. "I want a tiny nose and full lips and high cheekbones. I want long, dark eyelashes and nice eyebrows. I don't want to look like Mrs. Mix-and-Match anymore."

Eleanor laughed her tinkly laugh again. "I can do this for you, Sarah, but you have to understand, it's a big change. You can look in the mirror and see longer legs or a curvier figure, and they just look like you've grown. Faster than expected, maybe, but still, growth is normal for a child. It is something you know will happen. All your life, though, you've looked in the mirror, seen your face, and said, 'That's me.' It is true that your face changes some as you grow, but it is still recognizable as you. To see a totally different face as your reflection can be quite a shock."

"It's a shock I want," Sarah said. "I hate my face the way it is."

"Very well, Sarah," Eleanor said, looking into her eyes. "As long as you're sure."

After Sarah ate dinner with her mom and did her homework, she showered and got ready for Eleanor to put her to sleep one more time. But as she snuggled under the covers, a disturbing thought occurred to her. "Eleanor?"

"Yes, Sarah?" She was already standing beside Sarah's bed.

"What will my mom think if I sit down to eat breakfast in the morning and I have a totally different face?"

Eleanor sat down on the bed. "It is a good question, Sarah, but she won't notice, not really. She may think you look especially rested or well, but she won't notice that your plain face has been replaced by a beautiful one. Mothers always think their children are beautiful, so when your mother looks at you, she has always seen great beauty."

"Oh, okay," Sarah said, feeling relaxed again. No wonder her mother didn't understand her problems. She thought her daughter was already beautiful. "I'm ready, then."

Eleanor touched Sarah's heart pendant. "And you remember—"

"That I always have to wear it and can never, ever take it off. Yes, I remember."

"Good." Eleanor stroked Sarah's hair and sang one more time,

*Go to sleep, go to sleep,*
*Go to sleep, my sweet Sarah,*
*When you wake, when you wake,*
*All your dreams will come true.*

Just like before, Sarah felt the changes before she saw them. As soon as she woke, she reached up and touched her nose. She felt not a potato-like bulb, but a pert little point. She ran her hands over the sides of her face and felt clearly defined cheekbones. She touched her lips and found them plumper than before. She hopped out of bed to take a look.

It was amazing. The person looking back at Sarah was a totally different person than before. Eleanor was right: It was shocking. But it was a good kind of shock. Everything she had hated about her appearance was gone and had been replaced by absolute perfection. Her eyes were wide and a deeper blue and fringed with long, sooty lashes. Her eyebrows were delicate arches. Her nose was tiny and perfectly straight, and her lips were a pink Cupid's bow. Her hair, while still brown, was fuller and shinier and fell into pretty, soft waves. She looked herself up and down. She smiled at herself with her straight, white teeth. Beautiful. She was the total package.

She surveyed the clothes in her closet. None of them seemed worthy of her new beauty. Maybe when Mom took her shopping for bras, they could also pick out a few outfits. After a lot of deliberation, she finally chose a red dress she'd bought on a whim but could never find the courage to wear. Now, though, she deserved to be the center of attention.

School was a totally new experience. She could feel everybody's eyes on her, guys and girls alike. When she looked at the Beautifuls, who also happened to be wearing red today, they looked back at her, not with disdain, but with interest.

At lunch, she mouthed *hi* at Abby, then walked straight to where the Beautifuls were sitting. This time she didn't sit right down at their table but made a show of casually wandering past it.

"Hey, New Girl," Lydia called. "You want to sit with us?"

She wasn't remotely a New Girl to the school, but she was a New Girl in her looks. "Sure, thanks," she said. She tried to sound casual, like it didn't make any difference to her whether she sat with them or with somebody else, but inside she was so excited she was turning cartwheels.

All the Beautifuls were eating salads just like she was.

"So," Lydia said, "what's your name?"

"Sarah." She had hoped Sarah was a name they found acceptable. It wasn't too bad. It wasn't like Hilda or Bertha or anything.

"I'm Lydia." Lydia tossed her lustrous blonde hair. She was so pretty—pretty enough to be a model. She would fit right in with the pictures on the walls of Sarah's room. "And this is Jillian, Tabitha, and Emma."

They needed no introduction, of course, but Sarah said "hi" like she had never seen them before.

"So," Lydia said, "who's your dress by?"

Sarah had watched enough fashion shows on TV to know Lydia was asking about the designer. "It's from Saks Fifth Avenue," she said. It was true. The label of the dress did read SAKS FIFTH AVENUE. However, Sarah and her mom had bought it at a local thrift store. Her mom was so excited when they found it. She loved thrifting.

"How often do you get to New York?" Lydia asked.

"Once or twice a year," Sarah lied. She had been to New York once when she was eleven. She and her mom had seen a Broadway show, ridden a ferry to the Statue of Liberty, and gone up in the Empire State Building. They had done no shopping in fancy stores. The only clothing Sarah had bought was an I LOVE NEW YORK T-shirt at a souvenir shop. A few washings had worn it as thin as tissue paper, but she still slept in it sometimes.

"So, Sarah," Emma said, regarding her with doe-like brown eyes, "what do your mom and dad do for a living?"

Sarah tried not to bristle visibly at the word *dad*. "Mom's a social worker, and Dad—" Before her dad had left Sarah and her mom, he had been a long-distance truck driver. Now she wasn't even sure what he did or where he lived. He moved a lot, changed girlfriends a lot. He called her on Christmas and her birthday. "He's . . . he's a lawyer."

The Beautifuls nodded their approval. "One more question"—this came from Jillian, the redhead with the catlike green eyes. "Do you have a boyfriend?"

Sarah felt her face heat up. "No, not at the moment."

"Well," Jillian said, leaning forward. "Is there a boy you like?"

Sarah knew her face had to be as red as her dress. "Yes."

Jillian smiled. "And his name is . . . ?"

Sarah looked around to make sure he wasn't nearby. "Mason Blair," she half whispered.

"Ooh, he's hot," Jillian said.

"Definitely hot," Lydia echoed.

"Hot," the other girls repeated like a chorus.

"So," Lydia said, looking Sarah over. "Don't follow us around like a puppy dog or anything, but if you want to sit with us at lunch, then sit. On Sunday afternoons we go to the mall and try on clothes and makeup, maybe get a froyo. It's lame, but it's something to do. This town's sooo boring." She yawned theatrically.

"So boring," Sarah agreed, but inside she was buzzing with excitement.

Lydia nodded. "We'll hang out a little and see how things go. If it works out, maybe you can go out for cheerleader next year. Consider this a trial period."

Sarah left the cafeteria smiling to herself. Abby caught up to her.

"It looked like you were having some kind of intense job interview back there," Abby said. She was wearing gray sweatpants with a bulky purple sweater that did nothing to show off her shape.

"Yeah, kind of. They invited me to hang out, though, so I guess I passed the test." She couldn't stop herself from smiling.

Abby raised an eyebrow. "And those are the kind of friends you want? The kind that make you pass a test?"

"They're cool, Abby. They know all about fashion and makeup and guys."

"They're shallow, Sarah. They're as shallow as a rain puddle. No, I take that back. They're so shallow they make a rain puddle look like the ocean."

Sarah shook her head. She loved Abby, she really did, but why did she have to be so judgmental? "But they rule the school. That's how it works. It's the beautiful people who get what they want." She looked at Abby's gorgeous brown complexion, at her striking hazel eyes. "You could be beautiful, too, Abby. You'd be the prettiest girl in the school if you lost the glasses and braids and bought some clothes that weren't so baggy."

"If I didn't wear my glasses, I'd be walking into walls,"

Abby said, with a little edge in her voice. "And I like my braids and my baggy clothes. Especially this sweater. It's cozy." She shrugged her shoulders. "I guess I just like myself the way I am. Sorry if I'm not fancy or fashionable enough for you. I'm not like the cheerleaders or all those models and pop stars whose pictures you have plastered all over your room. But you know what? I'm a nice person, and I don't judge people on how they look or how much money they have, and I don't have to give a person a pop quiz to decide if I'll let them hang out with me or not!" Abby looked at Sarah's face searchingly. "You have changed, Sarah. And not for the better." Abby turned her back on Sarah and marched down the hall.

Sarah knew Abby was a little mad at her. But she also knew an apology and a hug would fix things once she'd had time to cool down.

After the bell, walking toward the school bus, Sarah became suddenly aware of a presence beside her.

"Hi," a male voice said.

She turned to see Mason Blair, looking perfect in a blue shirt that brought out the color of his eyes. "Oh . . . hi."

"So Lydia said you guys were talking about me in the cafeteria today."

"Well, I . . . uh . . ." Sarah fought the urge to run.

"Say, if you don't have anything else to do, do you want

to go over to the Brown Cow and have a cone with me?"

Sarah smiled. She could hardly believe her good luck today. "I don't have anything else to do."

The Brown Cow was basically a little concrete block shed that sold soft-serve ice cream and milkshakes. It was right across the street from school, but Sarah usually resisted the temptation of stopping there since she had always been worried about her weight.

She stood next to Mason at the counter where the same bored-seeming old lady always took orders. "Chocolate, vanilla, or swirl?" he asked her.

"Swirl," she said, making a move to open her purse.

"No," Mason said, putting up his hand. "I got it. It's a cheap date. I can handle it."

"Thanks." He had said *date*. It was a real date. Sarah's first.

They sat across from each other at a picnic table. Mason attacked his cone with gusto, but Sarah took tiny licks. She didn't want to eat like a pig in front of Mason, and she was afraid of the ice cream dripping on her dress and making her look like a slob. Even with her self-consciousness, though, she had to admit the cold, creamy treat was delicious. "I haven't had ice cream in ages," she said.

"Why's that?" Mason said. "Watching your weight?"

Sarah nodded.

"No need to worry about that," Mason said. "You look great. It's funny. You've been going to this school a long time, right? I don't know how I only just noticed you."

Sarah felt herself blushing. "You noticed me when I ran into you with that salad, right?"

Mason looked at her with his dark-lashed, ocean-blue eyes. "I didn't notice you then the way I should have. I clearly need to pay better attention."

"Me too," Sarah said, "so I don't keep plowing into people with trays of salad."

Mason laughed, showing those gorgeous white teeth.

Sarah was amazed by how confident her new looks made her feel. She could eat ice cream with a cute guy and make jokes with him. The old Sarah would've been much too shy. Not that a cute guy would've asked the old Mrs. Mix-and-Match Sarah out for ice cream in the first place.

Once they'd finished their cones, Mason said, "Hey, is your house pretty close? I could walk you back if you like."

Sarah felt a twinge of anxiety. Mason's dad was a doctor, and his mom was a successful real estate agent whose face was plastered on billboards. His family probably lived in a mansion on the fancy side of town. She wasn't ready for him to walk with her past the garbage dump to the plain little two-bedroom bungalow she shared with her living-from-paycheck-to-paycheck single mom. "Uh . . . I actually have to run a couple of errands this afternoon. Maybe another time?"

"Uh, sure. Okay." Was it Sarah's imagination, or did he look kind of disappointed? He looked down at his shoes, then back up at Sarah. "Hey, maybe we could go out for real some time. Pizza and a movie, maybe?"

Sarah was pretty sure her heart had just turned a backflip. "I'd like that."

His expression brightened. "How about this Saturday night? If you're free, of course."

Sarah fought the urge to laugh. Had there ever been a Saturday night when she *wasn't* free? All the same, she didn't want to sound too eager. "I think so, yeah."

"Great. We'll plan on it, then."

Sarah couldn't wait for Eleanor to wake up so she could tell her about her day. Finally, after what seemed like ages, Eleanor pivoted her waist and lifted her arms and said, "Hello, Sarah."

Sarah ran up to Eleanor and took both of her hands in hers. "Oh, Eleanor, I just had the best day of my life!"

Eleanor turned her head. "Tell me about it, Sarah."

Sarah flopped down on the bed and propped herself up on a pillow. "I hardly know where to start. The Beautifuls let me sit at their table at lunch, and then they invited me to meet them at the mall on Sunday."

Eleanor nodded. "That is good news, Sarah."

Sarah leaned forward and hugged the old Freddy Fazbear teddy bear on her bed. "And then Mason Blair took me for ice cream after school and asked me to dinner and a movie on Saturday!"

"That's very exciting." Eleanor stepped closer to Sarah, bent at the waist, and touched Sarah's cheek. "Is he a handsome boy, Sarah?"

Sarah nodded. She couldn't stop smiling. "Yes. Very."

"Are you happy, Sarah?"

Sarah laughed and repeated, "Yes. Very."

"Have I given you everything you wished for?"

Sarah couldn't think of a single other wish. She was beautiful and perfect, and her life was beautiful and perfect to match. "Yes, you have."

"Then I have everything I wished for, too," Eleanor said. "But remember, even though all your wishes are granted, the necklace still has to stay on. You can—"

"Never, ever take it off. I remember," Sarah said. She was always tempted to ask Eleanor what would happen if she took it off, but part of her was afraid to know the answer.

"Making you happy makes me happy, Sarah," Eleanor said.

Sarah felt tears welling in her newly beautiful blue

eyes. She knew she'd never have a better friend than Eleanor.

On Saturday, Sarah was a ball of nervous energy. From the moment she woke up, all she could think about was the date. At breakfast, she was too nervous to eat much even though Mom had made French toast, Sarah's favorite. "You'll drive me to the pizza place and drop me at six, right?" she said.

"Of course," Mom said, flipping through the newspaper.

"And you'll just drop me, right? You won't walk in with me or anything?"

Mom smiled. "I promise I will not endanger your relationship by letting your new beau catch a glimpse of my horrifying face."

Sarah laughed. "It's not that, Mom. You're really pretty, actually. It's just that it looks kind of a little kiddish when your mom comes in with you, you know?"

"I know," Mom said, sipping her coffee. "I was fourteen, too, once, believe it or not."

"And did you ride your dinosaur when you went out on dates?" Sarah asked.

"Sometimes," Mom said. "But usually I'd just invite the boy over to hang out in the family cave." She reached over and tousled Sarah's hair. "Don't be too much of a smart aleck, or I might decide I'm too old and decrepit to drive you tonight. Have you figured out what you're going to wear?"

At this question, Sarah let out a dramatic moan. "I can't decide! I mean, it's just pizza and a movie, so I don't want to dress like it's the most important event of my life. But at the same time, how I look is really important!"

"So wear jeans and a nice shirt. You're a beautiful girl, Sarah. You'll look great in whatever you choose."

"Thanks, Mom." She remembered what Eleanor had said about mothers always thinking their children were beautiful. She knew that her mom would've said the same thing to her even before she got Eleanor's help.

When Sarah's mom pulled into the parking lot of the Pizza Palazzo, Sarah's stomach was so full of butterflies that she couldn't imagine there would be any room for pizza. She knew she looked nice, though, so that was some comfort.

"Text me when the movie's over, and I'll come get you," Mom said. She reached over and squeezed Sarah's hand. "And have fun."

"I'll try," Sarah said. Until recently, the idea of going out with Mason Blair would have been as realistic as the idea of her going out with a major pop star. It had been a fantasy, something she dreamed of but never imagined would come true. Why was she so nervous when this was something she'd wanted for so long? Maybe that's what was making her nervous . . . the fact that she wanted it so much.

But when she walked through the doorway of the Pizza Palazzo and saw Mason waiting for her in front of the hostess's station, she immediately felt more at ease. He stood up and flashed his gorgeous smile. "Hi. You look great," he said.

"Thanks." She did think the turquoise top she'd chosen went well with her eyes. "You do, too." He was dressed casually in a hoodie and a T-shirt for some video game, but he would look great in anything.

After they got settled at one of the red leather booths with matching checked tablecloths, Mason picked up a menu and said, "So what kind of pizza person are you? Thin crust? Thick crust? Any favorite toppings?"

"I'm a flexible pizza person," Sarah said. Despite her earlier nervousness, she was actually starting to feel hungry. "I pretty much just like pizza in general. Except for one thing. No pineapple on pizza, ever."

"Agreed!" Mason said, laughing. "Pineapple on pizza is an abomination. It should be illegal."

"I'm glad we agree on that," Sarah said. "If we hadn't, I probably would've just had to walk out of here and abandon you."

"And I would've totally deserved it," Mason said.

"People who eat pineapple on pizza deserve to be alone."

They agreed on a thin-crust pepperoni and mushroom pizza, and they chatted comfortably about their families and their hobbies as they ate. Mason had a lot of interests, and Sarah realized she probably didn't have enough of them. Before Eleanor, she had spent too much of her free time worrying about her appearance. Now that that problem was solved, she needed to branch out a little—listen to more music, read more books, maybe take up yoga or swimming. As a little kid, Sarah had loved swimming, but once she hit middle school, she was too self-conscious to let anybody see her in a swimsuit.

By the time she and Mason walked next door to the movie theater, Sarah felt like they were getting to know each other pretty well. He wasn't just cute. He was nice and funny, too. And in the dark theater, when he reached over and took her hand in his, it was the most perfect moment of a perfect night.

When she got back home and was putting on her nightgown, Eleanor quietly strolled up behind her and put her hand on her shoulder.

Sarah was startled but quickly recovered. "Hi, Eleanor," she said.

"Hello, Sarah. How was your date?" she asked.

Sarah felt a smile spreading on her face just from thinking about it. "It was great," she said. "He's gorgeous, but I also really like him as a person, you know? He asked me if I wanted to go to the basketball game with him next week. I'm not interested in basketball, but I'm definitely interested in him, so I'll go."

Eleanor laughed her tinny giggle. "So tonight, was it everything you hoped it would be?"

Sarah smiled at her robotic friend. "It was even better."

"I'm happy you're happy," Eleanor said, then moved back to her spot in the corner. "Good night, Sarah."

In the morning, Sarah found her mom in the laundry room. "Can you drive me to the mall to meet my friends this afternoon?" she asked.

Mom looked up from unloading the dryer and smiled. "You're quite the social butterfly this weekend. What time are you supposed to meet them?" She folded a towel and set it in the laundry basket.

"They just said in the afternoon," Sarah said.

"That's pretty vague, isn't it?" Mom said, folding another towel.

"I don't know. The way they said it, I kind of felt like I should just know when they meant." She was so shocked to be accepted, even on a trial period, by the Beautifuls that she was afraid to ask questions.

"Your new friends expect you to be psychic?" Mom said.

"You don't like my new friends, do you?" Sarah said.

"I don't *know* your new friends, Sarah. I just know they were girls who wouldn't give you the time of day before, and now they're suddenly inviting you to hang out with them. It's kind of strange. I mean, what's changed?"

*I've changed,* Sarah thought. *Just look at me.* But she said, "Maybe they just finally decided I'm a likable person."

"Yeah, but what took them so long?" Mom said. "You know what friend of yours I like? Abby. She's smart and she's kind, and she's straightforward. You always know where you stand with a person like Abby."

Sarah didn't want to tell her mom that she and Abby weren't speaking to each other currently, so instead she said, "Two o'clock. How about you take me to the mall at two o'clock?"

"Okay." Mom tossed at towel at her. "Now help me fold."

Once Sarah got dropped at the mall, she realized that Lydia hadn't said anything about where to meet them, either. The mall wasn't that large, but it was big enough to turn searching for them into a fairly difficult game of hide-and-seek. She could text Lydia, she supposed, but it kind of felt like in order to be accepted by the group, she had to figure out the way they did things without making a nuisance of herself. If she was only accepted into the group on a trial period, she didn't want to make any missteps. One false move and she would be back to eating lunch at the loser table.

After a few moments of thought, she decided to head to Diller's, the mall's most expensive department store. The Beautifuls definitely wouldn't be hanging out somewhere cheap.

Her intuition was good. She found them at the front of the store in the cosmetics section, trying on lipsticks. "Sarah, you made it!" Lydia said, giving her a crimson-lipped smile. As soon as Lydia smiled at her, the other girls smiled, too.

"Hi," Sarah said, smiling back. She really had made it, hadn't she? And not just to the mall. She had great looks; a gorgeous, nice boyfriend; and the friendship of the most beautiful girls in the school. She could never have predicted that her life would be this good.

"Ooh, Sarah, you should try on this lipstick," Jillian said, holding out a golden tube. "It's pink with sparkles. It would look perfect with your skin tone."

Sarah took the tube, leaned over the makeup counter mirror, and smoothed on the lipstick. It really was pretty on her. It matched the rosy nail polish that never seemed to fade from her fingers and toes. "It looks like lipstick a princess would wear," she said, studying her reflection with pleasure.

"It really does," Tabitha said, opening up a tube in a different color. "Her Royal Highness, Princess Sarah."

"You should totally get it," Lydia said, looking at her approvingly.

Sarah tried to subtly check the price on the lipstick packaging. Forty dollars. She hoped her shock didn't show. That was more than she'd paid for the outfit she was wearing. But then again, she probably couldn't buy lipstick in a thrift store. "I'll think about it," she said.

"Oh, go on," Emma said. "Treat yourself."

"I want to browse around a little more first," Sarah said, "since I just got here."

She didn't want to admit that the only money she had in her purse was enough to cover a frozen yogurt and a soda. The Beautifuls, however, bought lipsticks and eye shadows and blush and brow pencils, whipping out wads of cash or their parents' credit cards.

After they finished at the makeup counter, they went to look at formal gowns because, as Lydia put it, "Prom's just around the corner."

"Isn't it just for juniors and seniors?" Sarah asked.

"It's for juniors and seniors *and their dates*," Lydia said. "So if you can find a junior or senior to take you, then it's just around the corner." She nudged Sarah. "Too bad Mason's not older."

"Yeah," Sarah said. But she didn't mean it. She liked

Mason the age he was. Besides, she wasn't sure she was ready to date an older guy.

The dresses really were beautiful. They were the color of jewels: amethyst, sapphire, ruby, emerald. Some were sparkly, others were satin smooth and shiny, and others were translucent with lace and tulle. They took turns trying on dresses and modeling them in front of the mirror and taking pictures of one another with their phones. After half an hour of watching them with a sour expression on her face, a saleslady came over and asked, "Were you girls actually interested in buying anything, or are you just playing dress-up?"

They ditched the dresses and fled the formal wear department, giggling.

"I don't think that saleslady liked us very much," Jillian said as they walked out of the store.

"Who cares?" Lydia said, laughing. "She doesn't get to judge me. She just works in a store. She makes minimum wage if she's lucky. I bet she can't even afford to buy the clothes she sells."

They went to the food court and ate frozen yogurts and laughed about how naughty they'd been. "Do you girls intend to buy anything, or are you just playing dress-up?" Lydia said over and over again, mimicking the saleslady.

They all laughed, and Sarah laughed right along with them, even though she thought they might have been a little hard on the saleslady, who was just trying to do her job. Jillian and Emma had left the dresses they'd tried on in crumpled piles on the dressing room floor. Now the saleslady probably had to clean up after them.

But who was she to criticize the Beautifuls? It was an honor that they invited her out with them. It was glamorous and exciting, like she was a guest on a reality TV show. No matter what they said or did, she was happy just to be included. Yesterday her date with Mason had been perfect, and now she got to be out with the Beautifuls. How could she ever express her gratitude to Eleanor? Nothing she could say would ever be enough.

That night, when Eleanor sprang to life, Sarah jumped up and hugged the robot's hard little body. "Thank you, Eleanor. Thank you for a perfect weekend."

"You're welcome, Sarah." Eleanor hugged her back, and as always, the sensation was odd. There was no softness in her hug. "It's the least I could do. You have given me so much."

Sarah settled down happily to sleep, but her rest was disturbed by a strange dream. She was on a date with Mason, sitting in the movie theater, but when he reached over to hold her hand, it was not his hand she grasped but Eleanor's—tiny, white, metallic, and cold, the same hand she had grabbed to pull the robot girl out of the car trunk. When she turned to look at Mason in the seat next to her, he had changed into Eleanor. Eleanor smiled, revealing a mouthful of sharp teeth.

In the dream, Sarah screamed.

She opened her eyes to find Eleanor standing over her bed, her head lowered, staring at her with her blank green eyes.

Sarah gasped. "Did I make a noise in my sleep?"

"No, Sarah."

Sarah looked at Eleanor, who was standing so close to her bed that she was touching it. "Then what are you doing standing over my bed?"

"Didn't you know, Sarah?" Eleanor said, reaching out to brush back Sarah's hair. "I do this every night. I watch over you. I keep you safe."

Maybe it was because of the dream, but for some reason, Sarah didn't feel like letting Eleanor touch her. "Safe from what?" Sarah asked.

"Safe from danger. Any danger. I want to protect you, Sarah."

"Uh, okay. Thanks, I guess." She appreciated Eleanor's concern, appreciated everything Eleanor had done for her, but still, it was creepy for someone to watch you when you didn't know you were being watched . . . even if they were doing so with the best of intentions.

"I can stand by the door if it makes you more comfortable, Sarah," Eleanor said.

"Yeah, that would be great." Sarah was pretty sure she couldn't fall back asleep with Eleanor standing right over her like that.

Eleanor strolled over to the door and stood guard there. "Good night, Sarah. Sleep well."

"Good night, Eleanor."

Sarah didn't sleep well. She didn't know what, but something was wrong.

In the cafeteria, Sarah stood in line with the other Beautifuls as they waited to empty their trays. Lydia had texted the night before saying they'd all be wearing their skinny jeans today, so Sarah was wearing hers, too. She'd bought the jeans and a few tops and a couple of pairs of cute shoes when her mom had taken her shopping the other week. They'd also bought a few bras that did her new figure justice.

"Can you believe what she's wearing? She dresses like a preschooler," Lydia said.

"Like a preschooler from a poor family," Tabitha added.

With horror, Sarah realized the girl they were criticizing was Abby, who was emptying her tray ahead of them. True, Abby was wearing pink overalls, so the preschooler comment wasn't too far off the mark. But it seemed mean to reduce somebody's whole value as a person to the clothes she wore. "That's Abby," Sarah heard herself saying. "She's really nice. She's been my friend since kindergarten." She almost found herself saying *best friend*, but she stopped herself in time.

"Yeah," Lydia said, laughing. "But you've bought new clothes since kindergarten and she hasn't."

The Beautifuls all laughed, too. Sarah tried for a smile, but she couldn't quite manage it.

When it was Sarah's turn to dump her tray, she stepped on something slippery near the trash can. Her new shoes were cute, but they didn't have much traction. The fall felt like it took forever, but she was sure it was only a matter of seconds. Then she was flat on her back, right in front of the whole school.

"Sarah, that was hilarious!" Lydia said. "What a klutz!" She was doubled over, laughing.

All the Beautifuls were laughing along with her, saying, "Did you see her go down?" and "She hit the floor like a ton of bricks" and "How embarrassing."

In Sarah's dazed state, she couldn't really tell which girl was saying what. Their voices sounded distant and distorted, almost as if Sarah was trying to hear them underwater.

Sarah tried to pull herself up, but something strange was happening to her body. She heard weird clashing and clanging sounds and couldn't figure out where they were coming from. It didn't make any sense, but they felt like they were coming from inside of her.

She was shaking and jerking, and she couldn't make her body move the way it usually did. Her body was no longer under her control. She was scared. Had she hurt herself badly? Should somebody call her mom? Call an ambulance?

And why were her new friends not helping her? They were still laughing, still joking about how stupid she looked and how funny it was.

Then the Beautifuls' laughter was replaced by screams.

As if from a great distance, Sarah heard Lydia saying, "What's happening to her? I don't understand!"

"I don't know!" one of the other girls said. "Somebody needs to do something!"

"Get a teacher, quick!" another one said.

A terrible thought occurred to Sarah. She put her hand to her throat. The necklace Eleanor gave her—the necklace that was never, ever to be taken off—was gone. She must have knocked it off during the fall. She turned her head and saw it on the floor just a little more than arm's length away. She had to get it back.

A hand reached down to help her. Sarah looked up to see that the hand belonged to Abby. She took it and allowed herself to be pulled up into an awkward standing position.

When Sarah looked down at her body, she saw the reason for the girls' screams. Her body was changing. From the waist down, she was no longer a flesh-and-blood girl, but a jumbled collection of gears and bicycle spokes and hubcaps, rusted metal odds and ends. Cast-off, useless parts that belonged in a wrecking yard.

She locked eyes with Abby and saw her friend's horror at what she was, at what she had become.

"I—I've got to go," Sarah said. Her voice sounded different, metallic and harsh.

Abby held out the necklace. "You dropped this," she said. Tears sparkled in her eyes.

"Thank you, Abby. You're a good friend," Sarah said. She didn't say anything to the Beautifuls, who had all backed away from her and were whispering among themselves.

Sarah grabbed the pendant and ran as fast as her new, shambling, makeshift metal legs would carry her out of the cafeteria and out of the school. Home. She had to get home. Eleanor would know what to do, would know how to help her.

Sarah was still changing. Her torso was hardening, and when she ran she made squeaking noises like a door with hinges that needed oiling. She tried to fasten the necklace around her neck again, but her fingers had grown too stiff to manage the clasp.

As she hurried down the sidewalk with a clattering, shambling gait, people stopped to stare at her. Drivers slowed down their cars to gawk. People didn't look sympathetic or even just confused. They looked scared. She was a monster, like something that had been created by a mad scientist in a lab. It was only a matter of time until villagers started chasing her with pitchforks and torches. She felt like crying, but apparently the kind of thing she was becoming was incapable of producing tears. Maybe tears would make her rust even worse.

Her joints were getting stiffer and stiffer, and it was growing harder and harder to run. But she had to get home. Eleanor was the only one who could help her.

Finally, after what seemed like hours, she reached her house. Somehow she managed to work the key in the door. She clinked and clanked through the living room and down the hall calling, "Eleanor! Eleanor!" Her voice was a terrible metallic scraping.

Eleanor was not in her usual corner of Sarah's room. Sarah searched the closet, looked under the bed, opened the chest at the foot of the bed. No Eleanor.

Sarah clomped through the house, searching her mom's room, the bathroom, the kitchen, all the time calling Eleanor's name with her new horrible voice.

The garage was the only place she hadn't looked. She used the kitchen entrance, but doorknobs were getting difficult to manage. Finally, after a few desperate minutes of fiddling, she was in the darkened garage.

"Eleanor!" she called again. Her jaw was stiff, and it was

getting harder and harder to form words. Eleanor's name came out as *"Eh-nah."*

Maybe the robot girl was hiding from her on purpose. Maybe it was some kind of joke or game. She looked at the ceiling-high storage cabinet against the back wall of the garage. It seemed like a good hiding place. With some difficulty, she grabbed the handle of the cabinet door and pulled.

It was an avalanche. Clear plastic bags holding different objects with different weights and sizes toppled out of the cabinet and fell to the floor with a dull, sickening thud.

Sarah looked at the floor. At first her brain couldn't even process what she saw. One bag contained a human leg, another a human arm. They were not the body parts of an adult, and they didn't appear to be the result of an accident. Blood pooled in the bottoms of the bags, but the limbs had been severed neatly, as if in a surgical amputation. Another bag, stuffed with bloody, snakelike entrails and what appeared to be a liver, slid from the cabinet's shelf and landed on the floor with a wet splat.

Why were there body parts in her garage? Sarah didn't fully understand until she saw the small bag that held a familiar-looking, potato-shaped nose. She screamed, but the sound that came out of her was like the squealing of a car's brakes.

Behind her came a metallic, tinkling laugh.

Sarah's lower body was almost immobile, but she dragged herself around to face Eleanor.

"I made your wish come true, Sarah," the pretty robot said with another metallic giggle. "And in return . . ."

Sarah noticed something she'd never seen on Eleanor before, a heart-shaped button just below Eleanor's throat that was a double of Sarah's heart-shaped pendant.

Eleanor laughed again, then pushed the heart-shaped button. She jerked and shook, but she also visibly softened, her silver finish turning the pinkish shade of Caucasian skin. In a matter of moments, she was a dead ringer for Sarah. The old Sarah. The real Sarah. The Sarah who, looking back on it, hadn't been so bad-looking after all. The Sarah who had spent way, way too much time worrying about her appearance.

Abby had been right. She had been right about a lot of things.

Eleanor pulled on an old pair of Sarah's jeans, one of her sweaters, and her tennis shoes. "Well, you certainly made *my* wishes come true," Eleanor said, smiling with Sarah's old smile. She pushed the button that opened the garage door. Sunlight flooded the room, and Eleanor-Sarah gave a little wave, then skipped out into the sunshine and down the sidewalk.

Sarah's ears filled with a deafening clinking and clanking. She couldn't control her movements. Different rusted metal parts disconnected from her and fell clattering to the floor. She was falling apart, collapsing into an ugly trash heap, a hideous, useless collection of garbage to be thrown away and forgotten. In an old mirror propped up against the garage wall, she saw herself. She was no longer a pretty girl, or a girl at all. She didn't resemble a human of any kind. She was nothing but a rusty, dirty pile of junk.

She felt sad; then she felt scared. And then she felt nothing at all.

# COUNT THE WAYS

**W**hy if it isn't Millie Fitzsimmons!" a deep, booming voice said. In the darkness, it was hard to tell exactly where it was coming from, but it felt like it was all around her. "Silly Millie, Chilly Millie, the ice-cold Goth girl who's always dreaming of Death. Am I right?"

"Who are you?" Millie demanded. "Where are you?"

Above her, a large pair of terrifying blue eyes rolled backward, looking down into the chamber.

"I'm right here, Silly Millie. Or maybe I should say *you're* right here. You're right inside my belly. In the belly of the beast, I guess you could say."

"So . . . you're the bear?" Millie wondered if she had fallen asleep after she climbed inside the old robot, if she was dreaming. This was all too weird.

"You can just think of me as a friend. Your friend till the end. We just have to decide if the end is going to be slow or quick."

"I—I don't understand." The space was starting to feel claustrophobic. She tried the door. It wouldn't budge.

"You'll understand very soon, Chilly Millie. You Goth girls crack me up . . . all dressed like professional mourners, so serious all the time. Daydreaming about Death like he's the lead singer of some boy band and that when you meet him it'll be love at first sight. Well, Merry Christmas, Millie! I'm going to make your dreams come true. It's not a question of 'if' but 'how.'"

What was happening? She was definitely awake. Had she lost her mind, descended into madness like a character in an Edgar Allan Poe story? "I—I'd like to get out now," she said. Her voice sounded small and shaky.

"Nonsense!" the voice said. "You're going to stay in here, all nice and cozy, while we work out how you're going to have your dream date with Death. The choice is all yours, but it will be my pleasure to present you with some options."

"Options of how to die?" Millie felt the cold, metallic taste of fear in the back of her throat. Fantasies about death were one thing, but this felt like reality.

Millie. What a stupid name. She was named after her great-grandmother Millicent Fitzsimmons. But Millie wasn't the kind of name you saddled a person with. A cat or a dog, maybe, but not an actual human.

Millie's black cat was named Annabel Lee after the beautiful dead girl in the Edgar Allan Poe poem, which meant that Millie's cat officially had a better name than she did.

But, Millie thought, it made sense that her parents would come up with such a ridiculous name. She loved them, but they were ridiculous people in a lot of ways, flighty and impractical, the kind of people who would never think how hard elementary school would be for a little girl whose name rhymed with *silly*. Her parents flitted from job to job, from hobby to hobby, and now, it seemed, from country to country.

Over the summer, Millie's dad had been offered a one-year teaching job in Saudi Arabia. Her mom and dad had given her a choice: She could go with them ("It'll be an adventure!" her mom kept saying) and be homeschooled. Or she could move in with her kooky grandpa for the year and start at the local high school.

Talk about a lose-lose situation.

After lots of crying and raging and sulking, Millie had finally chosen the Kooky Grandpa Option over being stranded in a foreign country with her well-meaning but unreliable parents.

And so now Millie was here in her strange little room in Grandpa's big, strange Victorian house. She had to admit, the idea of living in an old, sprawling 150-year-old house, where surely *someone* had to have died at some point, suited her well enough. The only problem was that it was filled to the brim with her grandparents' junk.

Millie's grandpa was a collector. Lots of people have collections, of course—comic books or gaming cards or action figures. But Grandpa didn't collect a specific type of thing so much as accumulate a lot of different things. He was definitely a collector, but a collector of what, Millie wasn't sure. It all seemed very random. Looking around the living room, she could see old license plates and hubcaps hanging on one wall, old baseball bats and tennis rackets on another. A life-size suit of armor stood guard at one side of the front door, and a mangy-looking taxidermy bobcat stood at the other side, its mouth open and fangs bared in a menacing fashion. One glass case in the living room contained nothing but old porcelain baby dolls with tiny teeth and staring glass eyes. They were creepy, and Millie tried to stay away from them, though they still showed up sometimes in her nightmares with those little teeth chomping at her.

Her new bedroom had been her grandma's sewing room, and it still contained the old sewing machine even though her grandma had died before Millie was born. Grandpa had moved in a narrow bed and a dresser to accommodate Millie and her belongings, and she had tried to make the room her own. She draped the bedside lamp with a sheer black lacy scarf so it gave off a muted glow. She covered the dresser with dripping candles, and she hung posters of Curt Carrion, her favorite singer, on the walls.

In one poster, the cover design for his album *Rigor Mortis,* Curt's lips were peeled back to reveal a set of metal fangs. A perfect red bead of blood glistened on his chin.

The trouble was, though, that no matter how much Millie tried to match the room's decor to her personality, it never quite worked. The sewing machine was there, and the wallpaper was cream-colored and decorated with tiny pink rosebuds. Even with Curt Carrion's fanged face glowering on the wall, there was something about the room that seemed sweet and old ladyish.

"Soup's on!" Grandpa called from the bottom of the stairs. This was how he always announced dinner, and yet he had never once served soup.

"I'll be there in a minute," Millie yelled back. Not really caring whether she ate dinner or not, she dragged herself off the bed and made her way downstairs slowly, trying not to bump into or trip over any of the clutter that seemed to fill every square inch of space in the house.

Millie met Grandpa in the dining room, where the walls were decorated with souvenir plates printed with the names and landmarks of different states he had visited with Grandma when she was alive. The opposite wall displayed replicas of antique swords. Millie wasn't sure what those were about.

Grandpa was every bit as weird as his collections. His wispy gray hair was always messy and wild, and he always wore the same ratty tan cardigan. He looked like he could play a wacky inventor in an old movie.

"Dinner is served, madame," Grandpa said, setting a bowl of mashed potatoes on the table.

Millie sat at her place at the table and surveyed the visually disgusting meal: mushy-looking meat loaf, instant mashed potatoes, and creamed spinach that she knew had been packaged and frozen in a solid block until he zapped it in the microwave. It was a meal you could eat even if you didn't have teeth, which, Millie supposed, went with the territory of having an old person cook for you.

Millie loaded her plate with mashed potatoes since they were the only edible thing on the table.

"Now make sure you get some meat loaf and spinach, too," Grandpa said, passing her the bowl of greens. "You need the iron. You always look so pale."

"I like being pale." Millie wore a sheer light powder to make her face look even paler in contrast to the black eyeliner and black clothing she favored.

"Well," Grandpa said, helping himself to meat loaf, "I'm glad you don't bake yourself in the sun like your mother did when she was your age. Still, you could use a little color in your cheeks." He held out the platter of meat loaf to her.

"You know I don't eat meat, Grandpa." Meat was gross. And also murder.

"Eat some spinach, then," Grandpa said, spooning some out on her plate. "Plenty of iron in it. You know, back when I learned to do the little bit of cooking I can manage, it was all about meat: meat loaf, steaks, roast beef, pork chops. But if you'll help me find some vegetarian recipes, I'll sure try to cook 'em. It would probably be better for my health to eat less meat anyway."

Millie sighed and pushed the spinach around on her plate. "Don't bother. It doesn't really matter whether I eat or not."

Grandpa set down his fork. "Of course it matters. Everybody's got to eat." He shook his head. "There's no pleasing you, is there, girlie? I'm trying to be nice and figure out what you like. I want you to be happy here."

Millie pushed her plate away. "It's a waste of energy to try to make me happy. I'm not a happy person. And you know what? I'm glad I'm not happy. Happy people are just lying to themselves."

"Well, if there's nothing in store for you but misery, I guess you might as well go get started on your homework," Grandpa said and ate his last bite of mashed potatoes.

Millie rolled her eyes and flounced out of the room. Homework was a misery. School was a misery. Her whole life was a misery.

In her miserable room, Millie opened her laptop and searched for "famous poems about death." She reread her old favorites, "Annabel Lee" (the cat with the same name was curled up on her bed) and "The Raven" by Poe, then tried one she'd never seen before by Emily Dickinson. The poem talked about Death as a guy picking up a girl for a date. A date with Death. The thought made Millie light-headed. She thought of Death as a handsome, black-cloaked stranger choosing her as the one he would take away from the boredom and misery of everyday life. She imagined he looked just like Curt Carrion.

Inspired, she grabbed her black leather journal and began to write:

*Oh, Death, show me now your ravaged face,*
*Oh, Death, how I long for your chilly embrace.*
*Oh, Death, my life is such a misery*
*That only you can set me free.*

She knew poems didn't have to rhyme, but Edgar Allan Poe and Emily Dickinson rhymed, so she rhymed her poem, too. *Not bad*, she decided.

Sighing with dread of what lay before her, she closed her journal and took out her homework. Algebra. What use was algebra in the face of human beings' inevitable mortality? None. Well, none except that if she didn't pass all her classes, her parents would cut off the allowance that her grandpa doled out to her every week. And she was saving up for more jet mourning jewelry. She opened her algebra book, picked up her pencil, and began.

A few minutes later, there was a knock on the door.

"What?" Millie snapped and slammed her book shut, as if she'd been interrupted doing something she actually enjoyed.

Grandpa nudged the door open with his foot. He was carrying a glass of milk and a plate of fragrant chocolate chip cookies. "I thought you might need a little study fuel," he said. "I know chocolate always did the trick for me."

"Grandpa, I'm not a little kid anymore," Millie said.

"You can't buy my happiness with a few cookies."

"Okay," Grandpa said, still holding the plate. "You want me to take them away, then?"

"No," Millie said quickly. "Leave them."

Grandpa shook his head, smiled a little, and set the plate and the glass on Millie's bedside table. "I'm going to putter around in my workshop for an hour or so, girlie," he said. "Call me if you need anything."

"I won't need anything," Millie said, turning back to her algebra homework.

She waited until she was sure he was gone and then devoured the cookies.

"Options of how to die. Exactly!" the voice in the darkness said. "You're catching on now, bright girl that you are. Now I'd call the first couple of options the lazy choices. They don't require me to do anything but keep you here and let nature take its course. The advantage to these is that they're easy-peasy for me but not so easy for you. Slow, with lots of suffering, but who knows? That might appeal to your morbid sensibilities. Lots of opportunities for languishing. You like languishing."

"What do you mean?" Millie asked. Whatever the answer was, she knew she wasn't going to like it.

"Dehydration is one option," the voice said. "No water at all, and you could start dying in as few as three days or as many as seven. You're young and healthy, so I'd put my money on it taking you a while. Depriving the body of water has fascinating effects. With no fluids coming in to filter and flush, the kidneys shut down and your body starts poisoning itself, making you sicker and sicker. Once those poisons have time to build up, you can suffer total organ failure or a heart attack or stroke. But that's death for you. So glamorous. So romantic."

"Are you making fun of me?" The voice that came out of Millie was tiny and soft, the voice of a scared little girl.

"Not at all, my dear. I like you, Millie, and that's why I'm here to make your wishes come true. Like a genie, except you're the one who's trapped in a bottle." The voice stopped to chuckle. "Starvation is another classic, too, but that's really a slow-moving train. It takes weeks for the body to use up its stores of nutrition and break down all its proteins and turn on itself. It can take weeks. Some people have even lasted a couple of months."

Millie knew her grandpa would rescue her before she could starve to death. "That'll never work. Grandpa comes in here to putter around after dinner every night. He'll find me."

"How?" the voice asked.

"He'll hear me in here. I'll scream."

"Scream all you want, lamb chop. It's soundproof. No

one will hear you. And anyway, after a few days, you'll be too weak to scream."

Winter break was just one week away, and the whole school was decorated with wreaths, Christmas trees, and the occasional menorah.

Millie didn't know why people got so excited over holidays. They were just a desperate attempt to invent some happiness in the face of life's utter meaninglessness. Well, they couldn't fool her. People could wish her merry Christmas and happy holidays until they turned Santa Claus–red in the face, but she wouldn't say it back.

Not that people were going out of their way to wish Millie well. As she walked down the hall to the lunchroom, one blonde cheerleader—Millie didn't even know her name—said, "I'm surprised to see you out in the daylight, Dracula's Daughter." The cheerleader looked over at her equally blonde friends, whom she'd been talking to more than she'd actually been talking to Millie, and they all laughed.

The Dracula's Daughter thing had started because she'd been carrying around a paperback copy of Bram Stoker's *Dracula*, and one of the jocky popular guys had said, "Oh, look, how sweet. She's reading a book about her dad."

From then on, she'd been Dracula's Daughter.

Of course everybody knew she was really Jeff and Audrey Fitzsimmons's daughter, which made her almost as much of a misfit as she would have been if Dracula were her real dad. The Fitzsimmonses were kind of a joke in the town, famous for their tendency to start projects with great enthusiasm and then abandon them. They had bought a run-down but once-beautiful colonial house when Millie was ten and had thrown themselves into refurbishing it. They had kept it up for about three months until they ran out of time, money, and energy. As a result, the house had a weird patchwork quality—the living room and the kitchen were repainted and had new fixtures, but the bedrooms still had old, peeling wallpaper, and floors with squeaky boards. The bathroom pipes screamed when you turned on the water and the ancient tub, sink, and toilet never looked clean no matter how much they were scrubbed.

The most talked-about thing, though, was the exterior of the house. Millie's dad had repainted the front and one side a nice, soft blue with cream trim, but paint was expensive, painting was exhausting, and he really didn't like getting up on ladders. As a result, the front of the house was painted beautifully, but the back and other side were still covered with old, flaking white paint. Millie's mom said nobody would notice. It was like when people arranged the Christmas tree so the ugly side faced the wall.

People noticed.

People also noticed the Fitzsimmonses' inability to keep a steady job. Millie's parents were always coming up with some new scheme that finally was going to bring them the success of their dreams. One year her mom was making candles and selling them at the farmers market, while her dad started a nutritional supplement store that closed its doors after six months. After that, her mom and dad started a store that sold yarn and knitting supplies, and they might have made a go of it if either of her parents had known more about yarn and knitting. And then they bought a food truck, even though they were both terrible cooks.

Millie couldn't understand how her parents could remain so optimistic with failure after failure, but they did. They attacked each new project with huge enthusiasm, and then after a few months, both the project and the enthusiasm fizzled out. They weren't poor, exactly—there was always food to eat, even if, toward the end of the month, it tended to dwindle to pancake mix and boxed macaroni and cheese—but there was always worry about how the bills would get paid.

Millie knew that her grandpa helped them out some months. Her grandpa was also considered weird in town but was cut some slack because he was old and a widower and had been an excellent high school math teacher for many years. As a result, he earned the title of "eccentric" instead of "weird."

Some people said that maybe by taking this teaching job in Saudi Arabia, Jeff was finally getting it together and following in his dad's footsteps. Millie knew, though, that her dad would fritter away this opportunity like he had so many others.

So Dracula's Daughter or Jeff and Audrey Fitzsimmons's daughter? Either one was a one-way ticket to being a social outcast.

In the cafeteria, Millie took a second to adjust to the deafening din of hundreds of teenagers talking and laughing. She walked past a table full of popular girls and saw her best friend from elementary school, Hannah, sitting with them, laughing at something all the other girls were laughing about. Millie and Hannah had been inseparable from kindergarten through fifth grade, playing on the swings or jumping rope together at every recess and playing dolls or board games at each other's houses after school.

But in middle school, popularity started to be more and more important to Hannah, and she drifted away from Millie and toward the crowd who was always giggling about clothes and boys. What Millie understood but Hannah did not was that those girls never accepted Hannah as more than a hanger-on. Hannah lived in a plain little house in a plain little neighborhood and didn't have the money or social status to make the cut. The popular girls didn't push her away, but they never let her into their inner circle, either. It made Millie sad that Hannah preferred to accept crumbs from the popular girls rather than real friendship from her.

But then, a lot of things made Millie sad.

Millie sat alone, nibbling on the egg salad sandwich and apple slices her grandpa had packed for her and reading *Tales of Mystery and Imagination*. She was managing to drown out all the cafeteria noise and focus on the story she was reading, "The Fall of the House of Usher." Roderick Usher, the main character in the story, couldn't bear noise of any kind.

But then she felt herself being watched.

She looked up from her work to see a lanky boy with horn-rimmed glasses and frizzy hair that had been dyed fire-engine red. Both his ears were studded with silver earrings. Millie coveted his black leather jacket.

"Hi, um, I was wondering,"—he nodded at the chair across from Millie—"is anybody sitting there?"

Was this guy asking to sit with her? Nobody ever asked to sit with her.

"My imaginary friend," Millie said. Wait . . . was that a joke? She never joked with people.

The boy grinned, revealing a mouthful of braces. "Well, would your imaginary friend mind if I sat in her lap?"

Millie looked at the empty chair for a second. "She says, 'Suit yourself.'"

"Okay," he said, setting his tray down. "Thanks. To both of you. I don't really know anybody yet. I'm new."

"Nice to meet you, New. I'm Millie." What, was she a comedian now?

"My name's Dylan, actually. I just moved here from

Toledo." He gestured toward her book. His fingernails were short but polished black. "A Poe fan, huh?"

Millie nodded.

"Me too," Dylan said. "And H. P. Lovecraft. I love all the old scary writers."

"I've never read Lovecraft," Millie said. Better to be honest than to try to fake knowledge and talk herself into a corner. "I've heard of him, though."

"Oh, you'd love him," Dylan said, dunking a cafeteria-issued chicken nugget into a puddle of ketchup. "Super dark and twisty." He looked around the cafeteria, his face a mask of disdain. "So is this school as lame as it seems?"

"Lamer," Millie said, marking her place in her book and shutting it. The House of Usher wasn't going anywhere, and she couldn't remember when she'd last had an interesting conversation.

"Well, I'll tell you what," Dylan said, gesturing with a french fry. "So far you're the only person I've seen here who seems cool."

Millie felt her face heating up. She hoped a blush wouldn't pinken her pallor. "Thanks," she said. "I, uh . . . like your jacket."

"And I like your earrings."

She reached up to touch one of the black teardrops that dangled from her earlobes. "Thanks. They're jet. Victorian mourning jewelry."

"I know," Dylan said.

He knew? What kind of high school guy knew about Victorian mourning jewelry? "I have a few pieces of it," Millie said. "I mostly find them on eBay. I can't afford my favorite kind, though, which is—"

Dylan put up his hand. "Wait, don't tell me. It's the kind where they weave the hair of the dead person into the jewelry, right?"

"Yes!" Millie said, shocked and amazed. "Those pieces show up sometimes on eBay, but they always cost a fortune."

The bell rang, signaling that lunch period was about to end. Dylan leaned toward Millie and half whispered, "Do not ask for whom the bell tolls."

"It tolls for thee," Millie finished. Where had this guy come from? Toledo, sure, but how was he so sophisticated and knowledgeable? She had never met anyone like him.

Dylan stood up. "Millie, it's been a rare pleasure. Would you and your imaginary friend mind very much if I joined you two at lunch tomorrow?"

Millie felt the corners of her mouth twitch in an unfamiliar way. "We wouldn't mind at all," she said.

"See, I had thought about freezing you to death, too," the voice said. "I thought I could short out the power in here so the space heater turns off, and my metal body can get pretty cold. But I figured your grandpa would come in and notice the power was out in his precious workshop and would fix it right away. So freezing to death is a no-go. Sorry if you had your heart set on that one, sweet pea."

Millie was shivering not from the cold, but from fear. "I don't understand. Why do you want to kill me?"

"Interesting you should ask," the voice said. "There are a couple of reasons, actually. The first is quite simply that it's something to do. I sat in a salvage yard for ages before your grandpa found me and brought me here, where I've just been sitting, too. I'm bored out of my skull. Not that I have a literal skull, but you know what I mean."

"Aren't there other things you could find to do besides killing people?" Millie asked. Whatever this being was, it was obviously intelligent. Maybe she could reason with it.

"None so interesting. And plus, there's my second reason, which is that death is what you want. You've been mooning around since you moved here, talking about how you want to die. Well, I like to kill people, and you want to die. It's a mutually beneficial relationship. Like those little birds that pick the parasites off rhinoceroses. The bird gets to eat, and the rhinoceros gets rid of the itchy little bugs. We both get what we want. Win-win."

Millie suddenly realized that she had spoken of death, written about it, but it had always been just an interesting idea to play around with. She never intended to take any action to make it a reality. "But I don't want to die. Not really."

A horrible rumbling sound surrounded Millie and shook the body of the machine that trapped her. It took her a few seconds to recognize the sound as laughter.

For dinner, Grandpa made spaghetti with marinara sauce, garlic bread, and Caesar salad. It was much better than the meals he usually slung together.

"You're actually eating tonight," Grandpa said.

"Because this is actually good," Millie said, twirling spaghetti on her fork.

"All right, I've finally found something you like to eat," Grandpa said. "I'll add it to my limited repertoire. I kept the sauce meatless for you and added meatballs to mine, so everybody's happy, herbivores and carnivores alike."

"Well, 'happy' may be stretching it," Millie said, unwilling to admit that she actually had kind of a good day. "But the spaghetti is good, and my day at school didn't totally stink."

"And what made the day less stinky than usual?" Grandpa asked, spearing a meatball.

"I met someone who seems kind of cool."

"Really? A girl someone or a boy someone?"

Millie didn't like Grandpa's insinuating tone. "Well, not that it matters, but it happens to be a boy. Don't try to turn it into some kind of love story, though. We just had a decent conversation, is all."

"A decent conversation is something, especially these days. Most people your age won't look up from their phones long enough to say as much as 'how do you do,'" Grandpa said. "Not to put the cart before the horse, but I met your grandma when I was just a little older than you are now."

"So what, now you have me engaged to this guy I just met? Grandpa, I'm fourteen!"

Grandpa laughed. "You're right that you're much too young to be engaged. And your grandma and I didn't get engaged when we were teenagers, either. But we were high school sweethearts, and then we went to the same college. We got engaged our senior year of college and married in June right after we graduated." He smiled. "And it all started with a good conversation at lunch, like you had today, so you never know."

"Slow down, old man," Millie said, fighting off a smile.

Grandpa's eyes went soft and misty. "I'm just reminiscing. I wish you could've known your grandma, Millie. She was really something special. And to lose her when she wasn't even forty—"

"It's like 'Annabel Lee,'" Millie said.

"The Poe poem?" Grandpa asked. "'It was many and

many a year ago, in a kingdom by the sea . . .' Yes, I guess it was something like that."

"You know Poe?" Millie asked. It was weird to hear him recite one of her favorite poems. Grandpa was a math person; she didn't expect him to know anything about poetry.

"Believe it or not, I'm a pretty literate old dude. I like Poe and a lot of other writers, too. I know you like Poe because he's dark and spooky, and it's easy to romanticize death when you're young and it's so far away. But Poe didn't write about death because he thought it was romantic. He wrote about it because he lost so many of the people he loved. You've never experienced that kind of loss, Millie. It . . . changes you." He blinked hard. "You know, for years after she died, friends were always trying to fix me up with other women, but it never worked. She was the only one for me."

Millie had never really thought about Grandpa's feelings before. How he must have felt when Grandma got sick and died. How lonely he must have been after she was gone. How he might still be lonely now. "That must've been hard," she said. "Losing Grandma."

Grandpa nodded. "It was. I still miss her every day."

"Well, thanks for dinner," Millie said. "I guess I'd better get started on my homework."

"Without being asked?" Grandpa said, smiling. "This is certainly a special day."

In her room, Millie didn't think of death. She thought of Dylan, and she thought about what Grandpa had said about Grandma. When she recited "Annabel Lee" in her head this time, it seemed like a poem about love instead of a poem about death.

"Silly Millie, for someone who doesn't want to die you sure spent a lot of time talking about it," the voice surrounding her said. "But that's the way of things, isn't it? Talk is always easier than action."

"I think," Millie said, sniffling, "that when I said I wanted to die, what I really wanted was to escape. I didn't want death. I just wanted my life to be different."

"Oh, but that really takes action, doesn't it?" the voice said. "Changing a life for the better, especially when the world is such a mean, rotten place? It's much easier—and ultimately much more satisfying—just to snuff it out. Which brings me to my second set of options. Much more interesting ones. These are quick and easy for you for the most part, but they require a little more effort from me. I'm not complaining, though. There's nothing I like more than a good challenge to relieve my boredom. Say, you like Dracula, don't you?"

Millie could barely find her voice to answer. "Why? Are you going to bite my neck?"

"Now how would I do that with you in my belly,

silly girl? I know that you're a Dracula fan. The kids at school call you Dracula's Daughter, don't they? Well, what you might not know is that the character of Dracula was inspired by a real person, a prince named Vlad Dracula. But he's better known by his nickname, Vlad the Impaler."

Millie's insides seemed to turn to jelly.

"Vlad killed thousands of his enemies, but his crowning achievement was creating a 'forest of the impaled' where thousands of his victims—men, women, and children—were skewered through stakes driven into the ground. Now I'm no prince and I can't aspire to that level of achievement, but one little old impaling can't be that hard, can it? I can just take one of my metal rods and drive it through my body cavity, and it'll go straight through you and out the other side. If the spike goes through your vital organs, death comes quickly. If it doesn't, there can be some hours of bleeding and suffering. The people who walked through the forest of the impaled talked about the moaning and gasping of the victims. So . . . impaling! One might say other deaths im-*pale* in comparison!" The voice's tone was cheery. "It can work quickly or slowly, but the result is the same in the end. Like I said, win-win."

"No," Millie whispered. She wanted her mom and dad. She wanted her grandpa. They would help her if they only knew. She'd even settle for goofy Uncle Rob and Aunt Sheri as long as they would come to her rescue.

She would even put on a Christmas sweater if it made them happy.

Millie sat at her table in the cafeteria expectantly. She had taken special care with her appearance this morning, choosing a lacy black top and a jet Victorian mourning necklace from her small collection. Her face powder enhanced her pallor, and her black eyeliner had the perfect catlike effect.

As minutes passed, she started to worry. What if Dylan didn't show up? What if she had gotten all dressed up for nothing? What if, as she'd always suspected, life offered no possibility of pleasure or happiness?

But then there he was, with his leather jacket and fire-engine red hair and shiny silver earrings.

"Hey," Millie said, trying not to sound like she was too happy to see him.

"Hey," he said, setting his tray on the table and sitting across from her. "I brought you something."

Millie's heart pounded in excitement. She hoped she didn't show it.

He reached into the pocket of his leather jacket and pulled out a worn paperback book. "H. P. Lovecraft," he said. "I was telling you about him yesterday."

"I remember," Millie said, taking the book. "*The Call of Cthulhu and Other Stories*. Did I say that right—Cthulhu?"

"Who knows?" Dylan said. "H. P. Lovecraft made it up,

and he's dead so we can't ask him. You can keep the book. I got a copy in hardcover for my birthday." He grinned. "My parents are cool. They don't mind that I like weird stuff."

"Thanks." She felt a little smile creeping up on her. She slipped the book into her bag.

She would certainly read the book, but it wasn't the book itself that was making her feel all smiley. It was that Dylan had thought of her. While he was at home, not in her presence, he had thought of her, found the book, put it in his jacket pocket, and remembered to give it to her. In her experience, boys weren't usually this thoughtful.

After dinner, in her room, Millie started reading the H. P. Lovecraft book. Dylan was right. It was weird. Weirder than Poe's stuff, even, and scary in a way that made it feel like spiders were crawling beneath her skin. But she loved it.

It was the perfect gift for Dylan to give her. Millie wasn't a flowers-and-candy kind of girl.

After she read a couple of stories, she opened her laptop. Instead of googling "poems about death," she searched for "poems about love." She found the famous one by Elizabeth Barrett Browning that began, "How do I love thee? Let me count the ways." She had read the poem before and thought of it just as pretty words, but now she could appreciate the feelings behind the words, strong feelings for the rare person who truly understood you and whom you understood in return.

She took out her black leather journal, chewed on her pen, and thought. Finally, she wrote,

> *You clipped away the black thorny vines*
> *That twisted around my wounded heart*
> *So it could beat and feel relief from pain.*
> *You are the gardener who wakes the plants*
> *From the gray, chilly death of winter*
> *So that they can blossom again like my heart,*
> *A slow-blooming bloodred rose.*

She read the poem back to herself and sighed with satisfaction. Her mood only darkened slightly when she set her journal aside to start on her homework.

"No? Pity. I always think impaling has a certain dramatic flair. Perhaps something with a little more zing? Electrocution is always an effective option. Did you know that the idea of the electric chair was developed in the 1800s by a dentist named Alfred P. Southwick? He came up with the idea of an electric chair based on his dental chair. That's not exactly comforting to people with dental phobias, now, is it? I don't have a chair to strap you into, but I do have the power to shoot a series of strong electrical currents through my body cavity. If the current zaps your heart or brain, you'll die quickly. If it doesn't, you'll have some nasty burns, and your heart will go into fibrillation, which will generally kill you if you don't have help. And I think we've already established that you don't have anyone here to help you."

*Help* was a word Millie wanted desperately to scream, but she knew it was a waste of energy—energy she needed to conserve if she had any hope of survival.

"So what do you think, cupcake? Electrocution? You'd be *shocked* at how effective it is. An *electrifyingly* good time!" Another chuckle.

Millie had once experienced a shock unplugging a hair dryer from a wall socket in a badly wired hotel room. She had felt the electricity tear painfully up her arm and for a few moments was as out of breath as if someone had punched her in the stomach. She didn't want to think about how an electric current strong enough to kill her would feel. "A good time for you but not for me," she said.

On Saturday afternoon, when most other kids were at the mall or the movies or hanging out at one another's houses, Millie walked downtown to the public library. It was about a twenty-minute walk, so the walk there and back with an hour or two of browsing and reading sandwiched in between was a pleasant way to spend a Saturday afternoon in solitude.

Today, she roamed the library stacks looking for suitably dark reading material. She had finished *The Call of Cthulhu* and was disappointed that there weren't any more books by Lovecraft on the shelves.

"Hey," a voice called behind her.

She gasped and jumped, but then saw it was Dylan.

"I didn't mean to startle you," he said. "Hey, did you read that Lovecraft book?"

Millie couldn't believe that the stars had aligned such that she had run into Dylan outside of school. "Yes, I loved it. I was kind of hoping they'd have more stuff by him here."

"Hmm . . . ," Dylan said. "I bet I can pick something else you'd like. Give me a sec." With a thoughtful expression, he scanned the shelves, then pulled out a thin book with a black cover and handed it to her.

"*The Lottery and Other Stories* by Shirley Jackson," she read.

"Yup, you'll love her. It's the perfect book to continue your classic horror pursuits. Hey," he said. "I was reading at that table over there until I saw you. If you want to sit there and read, too, you can."

"Okay." Millie worked hard not to show how happy this invitation made her.

"I've got to admit I've got an ulterior motive inviting you," Dylan said. "I want to see the look on your face once you finish reading the first short story in that book."

They sat at a table across from each other and read in companionable silence. Millie loved talking with Dylan, but being quiet with him was nice, too. She read "The Lottery" with a growing feeling of suspense, and when she got to the ending, Dylan laughed.

"You're reading with your mouth hanging open," he said. "It's the ultimate surprise ending, isn't it?"

"It really is."

"Say," Dylan said. "I was thinking that after I check out my books, I might have a cup of tea at the café next door. Would you like to do that, too? I mean, you don't have to drink tea just because I do. You can have coffee or hot chocolate."

"Tea sounds nice," Millie said. This afternoon was turning out to be nice. Surprisingly so.

Millie had passed You and Me Coffee and Tea hundreds of times but had never gone inside. It was a pleasant place with exposed brick walls displaying paintings by local artists. Sitting with Dylan over their steaming cups, Millie said, "I think I might like to be a librarian someday." She had never told anyone this before. She'd always been afraid of getting laughed at.

"That would be cool," Dylan said. "You love books."

"I love books, and I love quiet," Millie said, sipping her Earl Grey tea.

"You should totally dress in a Goth librarian style, too," Dylan said. "You could put your hair up and wear your jet jewelry and a black Victorian dress and those old-fashioned glasses that just clip onto your nose—what are they called?"

"Pince-nez?"

Dylan grinned. "Yeah, those. And when you dress like that and shush people in the library, it'll scare the living daylights out of them!"

Millie laughed, and she had to admit, it felt good.

School days were better when she knew she'd have lunch with Dylan. She could spend the morning looking forward to seeing him and the afternoon thinking about what they'd said to each other. Sometimes she felt a little silly for spending so much time thinking about a boy.

But Dylan wasn't just any ordinary boy.

Today, when she got home from school, her grandpa met her in the cluttered living room. "I thought we might go to the school holiday bazaar tonight," he said. Instead of his usual cardigan, he was wearing an ugly green pullover sweater decorated with creepy smiling Christmas trees.

"The holiday bazaar is stupid." Millie rolled her eyes.

"Just a bunch of people selling ugly Christmas tree ornaments made out of Popsicle sticks."

"Oh, I always thought the bazaar was kind of fun when I was a teacher. This year there's a chili supper and you can choose between meat and vegetarian chili. And there's an all-you-can-eat cookie buffet. Think about those words for a minute, Millie." He paused dramatically. "All you can eat. Cookie. Buffet."

"You've really done your homework on this, haven't you?" Millie said. She would never say it out loud, but it was kind of cute how excited Grandpa was.

"I have. I take cookies very seriously."

"I can see that." Millie sighed. Maybe just this time she could let the old man have something he wanted. The two of them didn't get out much, and it might be good for him to be among other people. "Okay, I guess I'll go even if it's not my thing."

"Great!" Grandpa said. "We'll leave in about an hour." He looked her up and down. "Maybe you could wear something besides black? Something, you know, a little more festive?"

"Don't push it, Grandpa," Millie said. She couldn't believe she'd agreed to attend such a lame event. But maybe Dylan would be there—under duress, like her—and they could make fun of it together.

The school halls were sparkly with Christmas lights, and

Millie had been correct in predicting the ugliness of the ornaments for sale. But the vegetarian chili was tasty, and there was an impressive variety of cookies on the cookie buffet, including gingerbread, which was her favorite. After she and Grandpa ate their fill, she wandered the hallways, giving the impression of looking at the craft displays but really looking for Dylan.

She found him in the second-floor hallway. But not in the way she wanted to.

Dylan was standing in front of a booth selling reindeer Christmas ornaments made out of candy canes. But he wasn't alone. He was with Brooke Harrison, a blandly pretty blonde girl who was in Millie's U.S. government class. Dylan and Brooke were holding hands and laughing about some private joke in a very couple-ish way.

Millie bit her lip to keep from gasping, turned around, and ran through the hall and down the stairs. She had to find Grandpa. She had to get out of there.

"Where's the fire, Dracula's Daughter?" some random kid asked her. She didn't even bother to process who it was. They were all the same anyway.

She ran into the cafeteria, scanning the crowd for Grandpa's ugly Christmas sweater. Unfortunately, a lot of people were wearing ugly Christmas sweaters.

She finally found Grandpa next to the drinks table, sipping coffee and chatting with a couple of other old men who were also retired teachers. These guys apparently shopped at the same ugly Christmas sweater store as Grandpa.

"We have to go," Millie hissed at him.

Grandpa knitted his brow in concern. "Are you sick or something?"

"No, I just have to go." Why wouldn't he move faster?

"Okay, honey." He gave the other old guys a look that seemed to say, *They're so emotional at this age*, and then said, "See you later, fellas. Merry Christmas."

In the car, Grandpa said, "What's the matter, honey? Did somebody at the school say something that hurt your feelings?"

Millie couldn't believe her grandpa could be so stupid. "Nobody at school said anything to me because nobody at school ever says anything to me. Nobody at this school cares whether I live or die!" She stifled a sob and wiped under her eyes to try to stop the flow of tears.

"I can remember feeling that way when I was your age. I wouldn't go back to being fourteen for anything, not even with all the years I'd get back."

The tears weren't stopping. Millie looked out the window and tried to ignore Grandpa. He couldn't possibly understand. Nobody could understand, especially people who got excited about Christmas sweaters and cookies and all that fake happy stuff they filled their minds with to ward off their fear of death.

Millie wasn't afraid of death. Right now, death felt like her only friend.

"My, we certainly are picky, aren't we?" the voice said. "For somebody who wants the end result, we're awfully fussy about how to achieve it. But there are lots more options. I feel like a waiter talking my way through the menu at a fancy restaurant. The difference, of course, is that one menu gets you fed. The other menu gets you dead." Low, rumbling laughter. "Oh, I crack myself up. Hmm . . . since I was talking about food, how about boiling? Did you know that Henry VIII made boiling alive the official form of punishment during his reign? Funny that they call it boiling alive because goodness knows you don't stay alive for very long. But I could easily flood my insides with water, then use my energy stores to bring the temperature up, up, up. First it would feel like a nice, warm bath, but then it would just keep getting hotter and hotter and hotter. I wonder if you'd turn red like a lobster?"

Millie sat miserably at her table in the cafeteria, knowing she was doomed to eat alone. She opened an anthology of horror stories she had checked out from the school library. Books, at least, would always keep her company.

But then Dylan sat down across from her acting like absolutely nothing was wrong. "Hey," he said.

"How can you just sit across from me like that?" Millie said. He was so casual, opening up his ketchup packets and creating a little red puddle on his plate, just like always.

"Like what?" Dylan said, looking lost. "I sit here every day."

"I would think you'd want to sit with Brooke," Millie said.

"Brooke has a different lunch period than me." He obliviously dipped a nugget into his ketchup puddle and popped it into his mouth.

Millie felt anger rising up all the way from her toes. "So I'm what? Your backup? Her understudy?"

Dylan rubbed his face like he was tired. "I'm sorry, Millie. I'm trying to keep up; I really am. But you're not making any sense."

Millie couldn't understand how he could be so stupid. "Dylan, I saw you. With her. At the bazaar last night."

"Yeah? So?"

She had never felt so exasperated. "You were holding hands. You were clearly together."

"Yeah? So?" he repeated. But then a look of realization dawned on his face. "Wait, Millie, did you think you and I were . . . dating?"

Millie swallowed hard and told herself not to cry. "You *noticed* me. Brought me a book. Took me out for tea. Of course I thought we might. In the future. Date, I mean."

"Wow," Dylan said. "I'm sorry if I misled you. I mean, you're really great and really pretty and everything, but I never meant to make you think we were anything other than friends. Haven't you ever had a friend who's a boy but who's not, you know, a boyfriend?"

Hannah had been Millie's only friend but had abandoned her. There was no way Millie was sharing this fact with Dylan. "Of course I have. But Dylan, you told me I was the only cool person you'd met at this school."

"I did. But that was my first day. I've met other cool people since then."

"Like Brooke?" Millie's voice dripped with sarcasm.

"What, you don't approve of Brooke?" Dylan said.

"She's blonde and basic," Millie said. No need to mince words. The truth was the truth.

"Have you ever had a conversation with her?" Dylan asked. "Do you even know what she's like?"

Had Millie ever heard Brooke say anything? She was quiet in U.S. government class, Millie assumed, because she had nothing interesting or important to say. "I've never talked to her," Millie said. "I don't talk to just anyone."

Dylan shook his head. "Well, Brooke isn't *just anyone*. She's smart and well-read and nice. She wants to be a veterinarian. Why does it matter what color her hair is?" Dylan looked at her so hard it was like he was looking through her. "Millie, I'm disappointed in you. You, of all people, with your black wardrobe and black eyeliner and black nail polish. It seems like you'd know better than to judge a person based on her appearance. You don't like when people do it to you, and yet you're guilty of the very same crime. I'm pretty sure that's called hypocrisy." He stood up. "I think this conversation is over."

As the winter holidays approached, Millie's mood became grimmer and grimmer. The cold temperatures and the gray skies and the stripped-bare trees all matched her emotional state perfectly. Cheerful holiday lights and plastic Santas on people's houses filled her with anger, and the sound of Christmas carols in stores and other public places enraged her. She felt that she couldn't be held responsible for her actions if she had to hear "Winter Wonderland" one more time.

Holiday cheer, peace on earth, and goodwill were just lies people told themselves. Winter was the season of death.

At dinner—vegetable stir-fry for Millie, chicken and vegetable stir-fry for Grandpa—Grandpa said, "So are you excited that tomorrow's the last day before winter break?"

"Not really," Millie said. "Listen, I've been meaning to tell you, I'm not celebrating Christmas this year."

Grandpa's face fell. "Not celebrating Christmas? But whyever not?"

Millie poked at a piece of broccoli with her fork. "I refuse to pretend to be happy on some particular day just because society tells me I'm supposed to be."

"It's not about society. It's about family," Grandpa said. "It's about getting together and enjoying each other's company. On Christmas Eve your aunt and uncle and cousins are coming over, and your mom and dad are going to Skype in so they can be a part of things. We'll have a big dinner and exchange gifts, and then we'll have hot chocolate and cookies and play board games."

Millie felt nauseous at the thought of all that false cheer. "I'll be here because I don't have anyplace else to go, but I refuse to participate in the festivities."

"Is that a fact?" Grandpa said. He pushed his plate away. "Listen, Millie, you've never been a particularly cheerful child. Heaven knows you were the fussiest baby I've ever seen, and when you were a toddler, your temper tantrums were legendary. But I feel like you're especially unhappy here with me now, and I'm genuinely sorry for that. I'm an old man and I'm no expert in what young girls like, but I've tried to make things as nice for you as I can. Maybe it would've been better if you had chosen to move abroad with your mom and dad. I know it must be hard to be so far away from them."

"I don't miss my parents!" Millie shouted. But even as she said it, she wasn't sure it was true. Sure, they made her crazy sometimes when they were together, but it was weird having them so far away, and Skyping with them on Sunday nights wasn't nearly enough to make up for their absence from her everyday life. It didn't help that she tended to be in a bad mood during their Skype sessions—mad at them for being gone—and so the conversations weren't always pleasant.

"Okay, maybe you don't," Grandpa said. "But something's been eating you lately—maybe a problem at school or a falling-out with a friend? I'm not saying I could help, but sometimes it helps just to have someone to listen."

Against her will, a picture of Dylan popped into her head—Dylan the first day she met him when she couldn't believe this cool new guy, who could've sat anywhere he wanted to in the cafeteria, chose to sit right across from her. Well, that never happened anymore. Now he sat at a table with those guys who never talked about anything but fantasy role-playing games, and Millie sat alone with only a book for company.

"I told you, I don't have any friends," Millie said.

"Well, maybe you should try to make one," Grandpa said. "You don't have to be a social butterfly if you don't want to, but everybody needs one good friend."

"You don't know what I need!" Millie stood up from the table. "I'm going to go do my homework." She didn't really have homework since tomorrow was the last day before break, but she'd say whatever she had to say to get out of there.

"And I'm going to my workshop," Grandpa said. "You're not the only one who can storm out of a room, you know, girlie." It was the first time since she had moved in with Grandpa that he sounded like he was actually mad at her.

In her room, Millie opened her laptop, went to YouTube, and typed in "Curt Carrion music videos." She clicked on "Death Mask," her favorite song. The video was filled with images of ravens and bats and circling vultures. In the center of it all was Curt Carrion himself, growling his way through the morbid lyrics, his black hair spiky, his complexion pallid, his black eyeliner perfectly applied. Millie felt like Curt Carrion might be the one person on the planet who would understand her.

Who was she kidding? Nobody would.

"Please don't boil me alive," Millie said. She had to figure out a way to escape. Suddenly, desperately, she wanted to live.

"Not boiling? Well, understandable. By all accounts, it is a nasty way to go. People who observed boilings during Henry VIII's time said it was so sickening they would have preferred to see a beheading. Oh! There's a good one we haven't talked about yet. Decapitation!" He said it like it was such a happy word. "There are many ways to chop off a head, of course, and if the blade is sharp enough, it's fairly quick and painless. That being said, if the blade isn't sharp enough . . . well, poor Mary, Queen of Scots, had to get three hacks with the headsman's dull old axe before her noggin was liberated from her body. The guillotine was quick and clean, though, and didn't require any particular skill on the part of the executioner, which made it easy to get rid of all those rich snots during the French Revolution. They just lined them up and ran them through the guillotine like an assembly line. Or rather, a *disassembly* line!" The voice paused again to chuckle. Whatever it was, it seemed to be having a very good time at Millie's expense. "Saudi Arabia—where your parents are, am I right?—still uses beheading as their preferred form of capital punishment. They use a sword, which I find rather stylish and dramatic."

*Saudi Arabia,* Millie thought. Her parents were so far away. So unable to help her. And now, as she was facing down death, she strangely felt more love for them than she ever had. Sure, they were weird and they made strange decisions and stupid mistakes, but she knew they loved her. She thought of her dad's awful jokes and of her mom reading her story after story at bedtime when she was little. Maybe her parents were different from other kids' parents, but they had always taken care of her basic needs, and they had always made her feel loved and safe.

Millie wanted to be safe.

"Millie, at least come downstairs and say hello!" Grandpa called up the stairs.

It was Christmas Eve, and Grandpa had been blasting Christmas music all day long, singing "Silver Bells" and "White Christmas" and others of Millie's least favorites off-key in the kitchen while he baked the ham and decorated the cookies.

From the level of noise downstairs, Millie assumed that her aunt and uncle and cousins had arrived. This fact did not fill her with joy. Nothing did.

Millie reluctantly dragged herself downstairs. They were gathered around an antique glass punch bowl that Grandpa had dug out from who knows where in this house full of stuff.

They were wearing Christmas sweaters, all of them, even her annoying little cousins. Aunt Sheri had on some wearable abomination with a reindeer that had a light-up nose. Uncle Rob, her dad's goofy brother, wore a red sweater with candy canes on it, and Cameron and Hayden wore matching elf sweaters. It was all so hideous that Millie feared her eyes would bleed.

"Merry Christmas!" Aunt Sheri greeted her, opening her arms for a hug.

Millie did not move toward her. "Hello," she said, her voice dripping icicles.

"Off to a funeral, Millie?" Uncle Rob said, nodding toward her head-to-toe black and purple clothing. He always said this to her and apparently never stopped finding it hilarious.

"I wish," Millie said. Better to be in an honest sad environment than a fake happy one. And she would certainly prefer funereal organ music to being forced to listen to "Winter Wonderland" again.

"Millie isn't celebrating Christmas this year," Grandpa said. "But at least she's agreed to grace us with her presence."

"How can you not want to celebrate Christmas?" Hayden said, looking up at Millie with big, innocent blue eyes. "Christmas is awesome." He had a little lisp that came out when he said "Christmas" and "awesome," which, Millie supposed, some people would find cute.

"And presents are awesome!" Cameron said, pumping his fist in excitement. Both kids were so hyper it was like their parents had poured them full of black coffee. Millie wondered if there had been a time when she got this excited over the holiday or whether she had always known better.

"Our culture is already too materialistic," Millie said. "Why do you want more stuff?"

Her aunt and uncle and cousins all looked uncomfortable. Good. Somebody in this family needed to tell the truth.

Sheri plastered a smile on her face. "Millie, won't you at least have a cup of eggnog?"

"Drinking eggnog is like drinking phlegm," Millie said. Really, how had such a disgusting beverage become a part of any traditional celebration? Eggnog and fruitcake both seemed more like they should be part of a punishment rather than a celebration.

"What's phlegm?" Hayden asked.

"It's that gross slimy stuff that's in your throat and nose when you have a cold," Aunt Sheri said.

Cameron raised his cup. "Yum! Egg snot!" he said, then took a big, showy drink that left an eggy mustache on his upper lip.

Millie couldn't take it. She had to get out of here. "I'm going for a walk," she said.

"Can we come, too?" Hayden asked.

"No," Millie said. "I need to be alone."

"Well, don't stray too far," Grandpa said. "We're eating dinner in an hour."

As Millie headed out the door, Grandpa called for her to remember her coat, but she ignored him.

All the houses in the neighborhood had extra cars in their driveways, no doubt because of visiting family members celebrating the holiday. All these people acting the same, doing the same thing. Presents and eggnog and hypocrisy. Well, Millie was different, and she wasn't going to participate.

*Hypocrisy,* she thought again, and this time the word stung her. Dylan had said she was a hypocrite because she judged Brooke by her appearance. But boys—even boys who seemed cool like Dylan—were fooled by appearances. If a conventionally pretty blonde girl paid any attention to them, they'd think she was a saint and a genius rolled into one. No way was Millie a hypocrite. She was a truth teller, and if some people couldn't handle the truth, that was their problem.

After one lap around the block, she was feeling pretty cold, but there was no way she was going back in the house yet.

An idea popped into her head. Grandpa's workshop had a little space heater he always kept running; it could keep her toasty warm while she waited out the party. He was too busy hosting his lame little holiday gathering to go into his workshop. It was a perfect place to hide.

Grandpa kept the key under a flowerpot beside the workshop door. Millie found it, opened the door, and pulled the chain on the bare light bulb that lit the small, windowless space. She closed the door behind her and looked around.

The place was even more crammed with stuff than it had been the last time she was here. Grandpa really must've been hitting the yard sales, flea markets, and salvage yards. Near his workbench was a rusty antique bicycle, the kind with a giant front wheel and a tiny back one. There were lots of old mechanical toys, too—a metal bank with a clown that flipped coins into its mouth, a jack-in-the-box that startled her when the jester doll inside jumped out, even though she'd known what would happen once she started turning the crank. There was even one of those horrible grinning monkey dolls that clanged cymbals together.

Why did Grandpa want all this stuff, and what did he plan to do with it? *Repair it and then use it to clutter the house some more,* she guessed.

The strangest item among many was tucked into one corner of the workshop. It was some kind of mechanical bear with a bow tie, top hat, and creepy blank grin. It looked like it once had been white and pink, but years of neglect had left it a dingy gray. It was big—big enough for a person to climb into its body cavity, like in those science-fiction movies where people "drove" giant robots. The hinges on its limbs made it look as if its parts had once moved. It must have been a figure from one of those old kids' attractions that featured creepy-looking animatronics. Why had little kids ever liked things that were nightmare-inducing?

From outside the workshop, Millie heard laughter and yelling. Hayden and Cameron, playing in the backyard. She hadn't thought to lock the workshop door from the inside. What if they tried to come in?

She couldn't let them find her. They'd go tell the adults, and then she'd be dragged back into the house and sentenced to mandatory celebration.

Millie found herself staring at the old animatronic bear, not just as a curiosity now, but as a potential solution to her problem.

She opened the door to the mechanical bear's body cavity, crawled inside, and shut the door behind her. Darkness enveloped her. It was so much better than those annoyingly twinkly lights and garish, bright Christmas sweaters.

This was perfect. No one would find her here. She could go back to the house after she heard Uncle Rob and Aunt Sheri's car pulling out of the driveway. So what if she missed Skyping with her parents? It served them right for being so far away from her on Christmas.

"Kids, time for Christmas dinner!" Grandpa called out the back door. "Millie, you come in, too, if you can hear me."

Cameron and Hayden came running in, their cheeks pink from the chilly air.

"It smells great in here," Cameron said.

"Well, that's because I cooked you a feast," Grandpa said. "Ham and sweet potatoes and rolls and your mom's green bean casserole. You boys didn't happen to see Millie while you were out there, did you?"

"Nope, didn't see her," Hayden said. "Grandpa, why is she so weird?"

Grandpa chuckled. "She's fourteen. You'll be weird when you're fourteen, too. Now go wash your hands before we sit down to eat."

At the table, Grandpa carved the big, sticky, beautiful ham. "I glazed this thing with Coca-Cola," he said. "Found the recipe on the internet. I've been looking up a lot of recipes since Millie moved in, most of them vegetarian so she won't starve herself to death. I bought this weird, fake turkey loaf thing for her at the grocery store. When she gets back, she can have it with the green bean casserole and sweet potatoes."

"I keep feeling like we ought to go out and look for her," Sheri said.

"Oh, she'll show up when she gets hungry or when she feels like she's made her point," Grandpa said. "She and that cat of hers aren't that different. She's just at that age, you know. Now, speaking of hungry, who wants some ham?"

"I don't have a sword like a Saudi Arabian executioner, Silly Millie," the voice said, "but I do have a sharp sheet of metal I could pass through the chamber. It could pass at the level of your throat, or it could hit you lower and bisect you. And bisection is a sure way to go, too. Either way, the job would get done! I think it would be smooth like Madame Guillotine instead of a slow, dull hacking like Mary, Queen of Scots experienced, but I'm not one hundred percent sure. This will be my first attempt at decapitation. Yours, too, but it will also be your last!"

As the voice laughed at its latest witticism, Millie pushed on the walls of the chamber that trapped her. They didn't budge. But then she saw a tiny crack of light shining through the side of the door. Maybe if she could slip something—a tool of some sort—into that crack, she could somehow pry the door open. But what could she use as a tool?

She took a mental survey of her jewelry. Her earrings were too small and breakable, and her necklace was an unhelpful string of jet beads. But there was the silver cuff bracelet on her wrist. She pulled it off and pushed and bent it until it was nearly ruler-straight. The end seemed like the right size to slip into the crack in the door. But she was too afraid to test it, too worried that her captor would notice.

"Millie?" the voice said. "Are you still with me? A decision must be made."

Millie thought. If she lowered her head and curled up into a little ball when the blade shot through, it would miss her. She'd have to be quick, though, and make sure she got her whole head out of the way, or else she'd get scalped.

If the blade came through lower to bisect her, she'd really have to flatten out in the bottom of the small space. "Is there any chance you would just let me go?" she asked. "Anything I could give you in exchange for my life?"

"Lamb chop, there's nothing I want from you except your life."

Millie took a deep breath. "Okay. Then decapitation it is."

"Really?" The voice sounded tremendously pleased. "Good choice. It's a classic. I promise you won't be disappointed." The low, rumbling laugh. "You won't be disappointed because you'll be dead!"

Millie felt more tears spring to her eyes. She had to be strong. But you could still cry and be strong at the same time. "Tell me when you're about to do it, okay? Don't just spring it on me."

"Fair enough, I suppose. It's not like you're going anywhere. Give me a few minutes to get ready. You know what they say—'Prior preparation prevents poor performance.'"

The chamber shook and rattled, then the animatronic's eyes rolled back outward, away from the chamber.

Millie waited, her heart pounding. Why had she ever wished for death? No matter how hard life could be, how depressing or disappointing, she wanted to live. If nothing else, she wanted the chance to apologize to Dylan for what she'd said about Brooke and to ask if they could be friends again.

She curled into as tiny a ball as she could, tucking her head under her arms. She hoped harder than she'd ever hoped for anything that she was low enough to miss the blade.

"Millicent Fitzsimmons, you are hereby sentenced to die for Crimes of Humanity."

"Wait," Millie said. "What does that mean—Crimes of Humanity?"

"You," the voice said, "have been rude and quick to anger. You have rushed to the judgment of others. You have been insufficiently grateful to those who have shown you nothing but love and kindness."

The voice was right. Different incidences of her own rudeness and ingratitude played in her head like scenes from a movie she didn't want to see. "Guilty as charged," Millie said. "But why are those crimes I have to die for? Those are crimes that everybody's guilty of from time to time."

"True," the voice said. "That's why they're Crimes of Humanity."

"But if they're something all humans are guilty of, then why do *I* have to die for them?" The voice didn't answer, and Millie felt a small tingle of hope. Maybe she wouldn't have to take her chances by curling up on the floor of the cavity. Maybe she could talk herself out of this yet.

"Because," the voice said, "you're the one who crawled into my belly."

Whimpering, Millie made herself as small as she possibly could in the bottom of the cavity. If she got out, she was going to make it a point to be nicer to Grandpa. He really had been good to her, taking her in and putting up with her moods and teaching himself how to cook all those vegetarian recipes.

"In the spirit of the French Revolution," the voice said, "I will now do a countdown in French before releasing the blade! *Un, deux, TROIS!*"

Quick as a shot, the blade sliced through the chamber.

Grandpa brought out a platter of sugar cookies and set them on the coffee table. "I'll be right back with the hot chocolate," he said. In the kitchen, he finally broke down and called Millie's cell number. Her phone rang from the pocket of her jacket that was hanging on the coatrack in the hall.

Oh, well. She would come back when she felt like she'd proved her point. He hated to think of her being outside without a jacket, though. It was pretty chilly out there.

Grandpa poured five cups of hot chocolate and topped them each with a generous handful of mini marshmallows. He carried the steaming cups on a tray into the living room. "Who's ready for presents?" he called.

"I am," Cameron shouted.

"I am!" Hayden shouted even louder.

"Do you think we should wait for Millie?" Sheri asked.

"She's not celebrating Christmas, remember?" Rob said. "Why should we wait for her if she's decided to be a brat?"

Grandpa didn't like the word *brat* being used to describe Millie. She wasn't a bad kid. She was just at a difficult age. She would come around. He crouched under the Christmas tree and arranged all her presents in a big pile so they'd be there for her when she came back.

# ABOUT THE AUTHORS

**Scott Cawthon** is the author of the bestselling video game series Five Nights at Freddy's, and while he is a game designer by trade, he is first and foremost a storyteller at heart. He is a graduate of The Art Institute of Houston and lives in Texas with his wife and four sons.

**Elley Cooper** writes fiction for young adults and adults. She has always loved horror and is grateful to Scott Cawthon for letting her spend time in his dark and twisted universe. Elley lives in Tennessee with her family and many spoiled pets and can often be found writing books with Kevin Anderson & Associates.

Propping his foot on an open drawer, Detective Larson leaned back in his wooden desk chair. Its typical creak sounded unusually loud in the absence of the daytime chaos of the divisional office. The bullpen was crammed with twelve desks, double that number of chairs, triple that number of computers and monitors and printers, a smattering of bulletin boards and storage cabinets and work tables, and the lone malfunctioning coffee maker stuck in the corner. The coffee maker spewed out abysmal coffee, but it made a musical hissing sound that a couple of the detectives thought sounded like "Ride of the Valkyries." It was on one of its more screeching crescendos right now.

Larson shook his head. He only noticed how depressing the place was when all the people were gone, as they were on this late Monday evening. He should have been gone, too, but he wasn't in a hurry to get back to his empty apartment. Ever since his wife, Angela, left him, filed for divorce, and embarked on a mission to be sure he saw their seven-year-old son, Ryan, as little as possible, Larson didn't see the point of going home. Home wasn't home. It was a two-bedroom walk-up that, according to Ryan, smelled like pickles and had the "ugliest carpet ever."

He'd told himself he'd stay late and catch up on reports, but he was really just sitting there feeling sorry for himself.

Was he really the horrible dad Angela accused him of being? Sure, the job forced him to miss a lot of Ryan's games and school events. Yes, he'd broken a lot of promises to his son.

"I'll be home in time to throw the ball, Ryan," turned into, "Sorry. I got a new case."

"I'll take you camping this weekend," turned into, "Sorry. The chief called me in."

"He's your *son*, Everett," Angela kept saying to him before she left. "He's not an afterthought. He should be your reason for being, not something you'll get around to someday."

Angela just didn't understand. He loved his son, of course, but this job wasn't just a job.

Yep, he was definitely feeling sorry for himself. Not the best use of his time.

Larson shifted, trying to find the ever-elusive comfortable

position in his desk chair. He looked around at the place where he'd spent two-thirds of his life over the last five years. It really was a bleak room. Dingy beige walls, flickering fluorescent lights, scuffed gray linoleum floor, all that furniture in perpetual disarray . . . *Were detectives so lowly that they deserved such surroundings, or were they just too darn busy to do anything about it?*

Larson shifted his gaze to the line of narrow windows that marched along the outside wall of the room. At the end of the row, he noticed a skinny ivy vine growing through a gap between the window frame and a dirty window that let in the sickly yellow glow of a street lamp.

"There's my favorite sucker."

Larson suppressed a groan. That's what he got for not going home.

"Chief," he said.

Chief Monahan wended his way through the empty desks, wrinkling his nose when he passed Detective Powell's monument to slobbery. "What is that stench?" The chief looked down at the piles of paperwork and empty food containers.

"Don't know. Don't *want* to know." From where Larson sat, the office smelled like disinfectant. His partner, Detective Roberts, whose desk faced Larson's tidy domain, sprayed the stuff incessantly to mask whatever it was that seemed to have died in Powell's desk.

The chief propped a foot on the extra chair next to Larson's desk. He held out an envelope. Larson eyed it. He had strong suspicion he wasn't going to like what was in it, so he made no move to take it.

The chief tossed the envelope onto Larson's smudged green desk blotter. It landed next to the row of freshly sharpened pencils Larson had lined up for his evening's drudgery.

"The Stitchwraith," the chief said. "No one else wants it."

"I don't want it."

"*Tough.*" The word sounded exactly that when the chief said it. A compact, prematurely gray-haired man, the chief made it clear early in his career that his size and hair color had nothing to do with his ability to kick ass. He wasn't big, but he could do what any big man could do. And he sounded like a big man, with a loud, rough voice you didn't argue with unless you absolutely had to.

Larson had to. He did not want to see what was in the envelope. "The Stitchwraith is an urban legend," Larson protested, still not touching the envelope, which lay like a big slug next to his foot.

"Not anymore. You heard the latest?" Chief Monahan clearly wasn't going to listen to dissent.

Larson sighed. How could he not have? It was all over the news, and the public was demanding answers.

A local teen, Sarah something, disappeared a week before,

and the detectives assigned to the case—not Larson, who gave thanks for small favors—had several dozen eyewitnesses who claimed the girl turned into garbage right before their eyes. Now admittedly the eyewitnesses were public school kids, not always the most stellar purveyors of truth, but in this case, their stories had a ring of authenticity, in spite of the outlandish content.

"I heard," Larson admitted.

"Can't make heads or tails of it, I know. But this morning, we had most of the witnesses back in to see the psychologists. The shrinks confirm the witnesses believe what they're saying. Same goes for the people who've seen The Stitchwraith."

Larson rolled his eyes then said in a deep voice, "'A strange cloaked figure roaming the streets.'" He returned to his normal unremarkable voice, "Did I go to sleep and wake up in a horror flick?"

The chief snorted then indicated the envelope with a shift of his square jaw. "You haven't heard the best part. Open it."

Larson took a deep breath and put his foot on the floor. He tipped his chair forward. It creaked again, this time louder, as if it, too, had no interest in The Stitchwraith and needed to voice its own objection. Larson picked up the envelope. Pulling an inch-thick stack of papers from it, he flipped through a few witness reports. Like the schoolkids' reports, these witnesses' testimonies all sounded similar, though they still had enough detail to diminish the possibility of a hoax.

The Stitchwraith, witnesses said, was a shrouded figure in some sort of cloak, cape, or hooded coat. It had a lurching walk, a complete disinterest in others unless bothered, and an obsession with dumpsters and trash bins. It was usually seen dragging garbage bags full of no-one-knew-what. He'd heard all of this before. He and most of his fellow detectives had dismissed it as bunk.

Setting aside the witness reports, Larson flipped through the next few sheets in the envelope. They were all suspicious death reports.

Larson kept his face blank as he read, and he was glad the chief couldn't see the frisson of dread that skittered along his nerve endings. He felt like the reports dropped a stone into the pond of his life, and now their impact was rippling inexorably outward toward some future he wasn't going to like.

Larson flipped through the stack. "Five? Five withered bodies with,"—he looked down and read from the top report stack—"'eyes that bled black down the sides of the face.' More of that?" The manner of death wasn't new to Larson, unfortunately, but he'd only known of one victim. And he didn't know it had anything to do with The Stitchwraith.

Chief Monahan shrugged.

Larson read more carefully. Two of the dead men found had impressive criminal histories. Larson recognized one of the guys—he'd collared him for assault a few years back. He separated out the two reports and tapped them. "I bet these two tried to mug the guy."

The chief, who had finally sat down in Larson's visitor chair, nodded. "I agree." He leaned forward and pointed to a stack of photographs Larson hadn't looked at yet. "Look at those."

Larson flipped through the photos taken from security cameras near The Stitchwraith sightings. He squinted at one that showed the figure pulling what seemed to be a mannequin's torso from a dumpster. "What the heck is he doing?"

The chief didn't answer.

Larson kept going through the photos. He stopped again. From under the hood of what looked like maybe a long trench coat, a bulky white face peered out at the night. Larson stiffened so he wouldn't recoil. He wanted to drop the photo and get as far from his desk as he could. But he didn't do that. He just stared at the strange visage and concentrated on breathing normally. He wasn't going to let this craziness rattle him, especially not in front of the chief.

The face wasn't a face, not a *human* face anyway. Unless it was a damaged human face covered in bandages maybe?

It looked more like a mask. The face was round, and its features were drawn onto the curved white surface. Done in thick black marker, the black features looked like a child had made them.

Larson deliberately relaxed his shoulders, which he realized had been creeping toward his ears. *It's just a stupid mask*, he told himself.

Larson looked up at Chief Monahan. "A mask?"

"Your guess is as good as mine."

Larson looked back at the face. It had dark eyes, one of which looked blackened, and it had a terrifying mouth with a missing tooth and something stuck between the remaining front teeth. Were those blood stains around the mouth?

"We got a match on it." The chief pressed his thin lips together in what could have been a smile. He liked dropping bombshells.

"A match on what? *This?*" Larson pointed at the blurred and bizarre face.

The chief nodded. "And you're not going to believe where we got it from."

# A DEADLY SECRET IS LURKING AT THE HEART OF FREDDY FAZBEAR'S PIZZA...

Unravel the twisted mysteries behind the bestselling horror video games and the *New York Times* bestselling series.